Impeccable Manners

by

Paul Budd

Speart House Publishing
Billesley House
Elgin Gardens
Stratford-upon-Avon
Warwickshire CV37 7BG

ISBN: 978-1-911323-23-5

For Toby, Oscar, Teddy and Jack

hoping humour will be part of their world

A Bad Influence

It was a Thursday, Ruth's bridge night. A chance to hobnob with everybody who is anybody she always tells me. Bit of a bore having to fend for oneself, so I decided that I'd stay late and finish the briefing I was working on with the Cabinet Secretary, and then rather than spend a quiet evening on my own with some ghastly pizza, I would pop into the club and have a bite to eat there.

I'd been a member for donkey's years. It used to be a favourite haunt for a lot of the foreign office johnnies, which came in handy before I moved to the Cabinet Office. I checked my coat in but kept hold of my briefcase, with the precious briefing inside, and went up to the library. There was no one else there. I ordered a drink and sat in an armchair in the corner of the room.

I was just enjoying my gin and tonic, looking through the menu, and facing a somewhat difficult choice between the partridge and the guineafowl, when I heard the door swing open.

'Guy Manners!' boomed a voice far too loud for the hush of the library. A tall, portly figure strode in, grey-haired and chin-first. 'What the devil are you doing here?'

It took me a few moments to recognise who it was. The voice was familiar but didn't seem to go with the body. Then, all of a sudden, it came to me, Charlie Hobson. I have to say that the years hadn't been particularly kind. The Charlie I remembered was a rather dapper sort of fellow, dark hair, blue eyes, always well dressed. The sort that only needed to glance in the direction of a young lady to make her blush. Charlie was someone that Ruth always defined as a "bad influence," a category she reserved for those of my friends who were prone to practical jokes, improbable financial schemes or too much alcohol.

'Charlie Hobson, as I live and breathe,' I said, rising to shake his hand. 'How the devil are you?'

'Not as well as you, clearly,' he laughed, patting his stomach and eyeing mine.

'My dear chap, do have a seat.' I indicated to a seat adjacent to mine. 'I'm a bridge widower tonight, would you care to join me for dinner?'

Charlie sank down into one of the Chesterfields. It groaned a little.

This seemed to me a splendid turn of events. Bad influence or not, Charlie Hobson had always been wonderful company.

'So, what are you up to these days?' I asked. 'Did that copper mine in the Congo pan out?'

'Went the way of all flesh,' he said, ordering a gin. 'There's a project in Tibet you might like.'

I thought about the colourful share certificates of The Bolivian Guano Company that still sat in the bottom my desk. It wasn't Charlie's fault that

guano is mostly found in Peru. 'I think my days of
overseas investment are long gone,' I said.

'Pity.' He took a healthy mouthful of gin,
'Anyway, I've been doing this and that. Still got a
small column in the Daily Insult that pays the old
out of pockets.' He grinned, 'Always interested in
any government tittle tattle. You still at the
foreign?'

'Cabinet Office.'

Charlie smiled, lean forward and raised his
glass. 'Congratulations old boy. Walking the
corridors of power hey?' He looked at my
somewhat depleted gin and tonic, 'same again?'
And, before I could answer, he ordered another
round.

We moved to the dining room. I placed my
briefcase between the table leg and my foot,
suddenly aware of its contents—notes on the
French President's visit and their maddening list of
demands. My scribbles in the margins were cryptic,
but still, I resolved not to let the case out of sight.

'How's Ruth?' Charlie asked.

'Very well,' I said, trying to recall his wife's
name. 'And Janet?'

'Doing well by all accounts. Married her Pilates
instructor,' he grinned. 'Did wonders for her spine.'

'I'm so sorry didn't work out.'

'Don't be. Pastures new old boy. Met this gorgeous creature, Xiu Mei.' He drained his gin and tonic. 'You know, the Chinese have such wonderful names, Xiu Mei means beautiful plum.'

I nodded and wondered what to say. Charlie was the same age as me and I couldn't quite picture him with some young Chinese girl, beautiful plum or not.

'I think I ought to pass, Charlie. Busy day tomorrow.'

'Nonsense old boy. Haven't seen you for ages. We should make a night of it.' He looked down the wine list. 'One of each, I think.' He ordered a bottle of Sancerre and a Merlot and smiled, 'Just like old times.'

As I took another sip of my gin and tonic, I caught sight of that rather disapproving portrait of Disraeli that hangs over the fireplace in the club dining room. For some reason I saw a passing resemblance to Ruth that I hadn't noticed before, possibly the way the arms were crossed or the slight pursing of the lips and, although I looked away, it seemed as if the eyes followed me.

A little disconcerted by the resemblance I heard Charlie ask, 'So do tell. What you make of this current shower?'

'Never right for a civil servant to discuss the weather,' I replied, pleased with myself.

'Hah!' Charlie laughed, 'you always were the diplomat Guy, but I know you. You must have a view.'

'Not one I can share I'm afraid.'

'Spoil sport.' He poured himself a glass of Sancerre and then reached over to fill mine.

The waiter arrived with my potted shrimps. I took a large sip of the Sancerre. It was crisp with a beautiful aroma of grapefruit and lilies and a light gooseberry tang that somehow made the potted shrimps taste better than any I'd had before. I took another mouthful of wine, savouring the cool burn as it went down and watched with surprising detachment as Charlie topped up my glass and ordered another bottle.

I thought how fortunate it was that I had bumped into Charlie. It was just like the old days. It was really good to see him, and I wondered how it was that we had lost touch. I remember asking if he still had that policeman's helmet, a trophy from a minor fracas that the George and Vulture and laughing when he reminded me what had happened to it later that night.

Charlie suggested we adjourn to the billiard room and have a frame or two of snooker. It seemed like a great way to round the evening off. We were almost out of the dining room before I remembered my briefcase. I bumped my head retrieving it but was relieved to have it in hand.

Charlie laughed. 'Careful old boy. Can't have you denting the furniture. What have you got in there anyway? State secrets?'

I ignored him. When we got to the billiard room, I put the briefcase on one of the coffee tables that are supposed to be out of harms' way of the players.

We racked the balls ourselves, arguing over the colour order. 'You Bless God,' I said. 'Bless You God,' Charlie insisted. The steward begged pardon before settling it: 'God Bless You.'

Lining up a long shot, my knee twinged. I ignored it. The rest wobbled. I misjudged the distance, slipped, and crashed into the coffee table. Papers flew everywhere.

Charlie was doubled up with laughter, but for the life of me I couldn't see what was so funny. I remember being annoyed, so much so that I forgot about my knee and, as I tried to stand up fell over again, compounding the damage to my knee, the briefcase and the coffee table. Charlie helped the steward pick me up, gathered my papers together and put them back in my briefcase.

The last thing I remember was a blur of black and yellow and a voice asking, 'Where to?' And several attempts to say, 'Richmond.'

I woke in the spare room, head pounding, knee throbbing. Ruth stood in the doorway, arms crossed, lips pursed.

'Well?' she asked.

'Not particularly.' I said, then realised that this needed some careful diplomacy. 'Cabinet Secretary decided to make a night of it.' Which probably would have been true if he had thought of it.

'George?' Ruth looked sceptical but unfolded her arms.

'Needed to sort out the French president's visit.' Which was almost true.

'Hmm, it's your liver Guy,' she said, and closed the door rather too loudly behind her.

In something of a panic, I remembered my briefcase but found it propped up against the bed. I opened it. All the papers were there, a bit the worse for wear, but nothing missing. I breathed a huge sigh of relief.

I won't deny that I have felt better. I couldn't face breakfast. The tube was dreadful. All that bumping, clanging and the smell a second-hand garlic and Steradent. I held on for grim death as far as Sloane Square but then got off and walked the rest of the way, breathing deeply.

When I got into the office I was surprised to see a message on my desk to call Charlie. I thought for one awful moment that I must, after all, I've left some of my papers at the club, but when I checked my briefcase again they were all there. I sat down and called the number on the message.

'Guy old boy! Just checking you got home safe.'

'Fine, fine. It was good to see you Charlie.' Waves of nausea started to wash against my ribs, and I took a few deep breaths.

'Hope you don't mind me asking old boy, but I'm writing my column for the Insult,' he paused, 'The notes you were splashing around at the club suggested the government are a bit ticked off with the old Froggies.'

The receiver began to shake in my hand. I could see my pension disappearing and the sort of hideous headlines that the Daily Insult specialised in.

'Why would you think that?' I asked.

'Well,' there was more shuffling paper, 'There's a handwritten note saying, "Hollande swans in – choice," and then some squiggles I couldn't read. Sorry to put you on the spot old boy but needs must.'

I tried to think of something to say. The French probably wouldn't give a fig about it, they knew what we thought anyway and would quite like to see us squirm a bit, but the PM would be livid. Think, think! Then it came to me.

I tried a laugh, which I hoped was convincing, 'Just goes to show how wrong you are Charlie. What you've got there is the PM's thoughts on dining arrangements.'

'On what?'

'Dining arrangements.' I paused, 'It's always a nightmare trying to find somewhere different to take important visitors.'

'I'm not with you.'

'That's what those notes mean.' There was silence at the other end of the phone. 'We'll be taking M. Hollande to a pub, the Swan Inn. It was his choice.'

I waited for a reaction. My palms were sweating.

'They're taking Hollande to a pub?'

'Absolutely. Man of the people. It's a sort of socialist thing.'

'Well, I'll be blowed.' I thought I could hear a hint of disappointment in his voice. 'So, where's this pub?'

'I'm hardly going to tell you that, am I?'

'Hmm. Well, I hope you'll remember your old pal when there's something newsworthy.'

I assured him that I would and put the phone down.

The following morning the Cabinet Secretary burst into my office carrying a copy of the Daily Insult.

'Have you read this?' He waved the paper at me.

'No.'

'The Insult's got it into their heads that the PM is taking Hollande to a pub called the Swan Inn for lunch.'

I didn't know what to say. It was like the proverbial hole opening up to swallow me. If it came down to it I could hardly deny that I was the source.

George opened the paper and pointed at the article. 'PM thinks it's a marvellous idea. Hollande can't refuse traditional hospitality, and it'll make anything we do later for Merkel look absolutely first-class. Inspired optics.'

I blinked. 'Really?'

'There's a Swan Inn in his constituency. You're coordinating it.'

I nodded, dazed.

The fate of Franco-British relations, sealed with a snooker cue and a second bottle of Merlot. Good old Charlie.

The Burning Issue

I have never liked golf, but I liked the fact that it
gave one an excuse to escape the office. One such
opportunity arose in July 2012 when I was invited
by Hugo Beaumont, an old chum from university
days, to the Open Golf.

Not only was it a good opportunity to escape the
daily grind as it were, but also a chance to avoid the
silly season. Not the silly news—Heaven knows
there was always enough of that—but avoiding the
hoary old chestnuts that somehow manage to
escape from the long grass while all the sensible
people are taking the summer off, and junior
politicians are left in charge. You know the sort of
thing; whether England should have its own
National Anthem; the UK's asteroid risk mitigation
strategy; whether Britain should adopt British
Summer Time all year round; strategies for
combatting methane pollution from cows.

They sound trivial, I know, but I remember poor
old Henry Binks getting caught on the National
Anthem issue for years until it was finally buried
again. Tried all the usual things; passing it on to the
Home Office; deferring it for consultation with
Scotland and Wales; but nothing worked. Left it for
his successor who, in desperation, finally stopped
sending out progress reports and people forgot all
about it. It's still there waiting for some naïve but
enthusiastic cabinet minister to wave their strimmer
in the wrong direction and bring the whole bally

thing back into play. Binky was never the same; started humming Land of Hope and Glory all the time, then took early retirement and bought a guest house on the Isle of Wight.

No, much better, I thought, to be away from it all. As luck would have it the Open was at Lytham St Annes; had to look it up on the map. A trifle too close to Blackpool for comfort, but that might well be a good thing, most sensible chaps would be heading for the continent or the South Coast.

As I got into the first class compartment at Euston, put my small overnight bag into the overhead rack, settled back to read the Times and enjoy a decent breakfast, I have to say I was feeling a little pleased with myself; not only was I escaping to the open, but I'd managed to wangle my way onto one of the Olympics committees; a difficult role ensuring compliance with Government policy in relation to overseas VIP arrangements that would require my regular attendance at various venues. With any luck I would be out of circulation until the autumn.

Odd sort of place, Lytham St Anne's. Hugo had put us up in some Victorian hotel in the town, a rather decent pile. You know the sort of thing, all gothic red brick on the outside and polished marble on the inside. I had a view out to the sea. Well, I say the sea, but you would have a long walk over the flats to reach the sea at low tide. Whole place looked like something out of a Dickens novel with geriatric donkeys hauling bored looking children along the beach; a deserted cast iron bandstand; and a rather fragile looking pier and beach huts. Never really understood beach huts myself, pokey little sheds that get unbearably hot during the day and don't have anything in them but a kettle and two deckchairs. Still *chacun a son gout* as they say, although probably not in Lytham St Annes, and I imagine that the beach huts provide some shelter from a persistent wind that the locals insist on describing as bracing in that cheery Fred Flintoff sort of way.

The hotel had what they described as a shuttle service to the golf course; a service I was fortunate enough to have to myself for the outward journey. The shuttle turned out to be a rather weathered transit van driven by a native of the area. I clambered into the rear of the van, taking care not to get my blazer too close to the spare tyre that, for some unknown reason, occupied the back seat. The driver displayed an impressive familiarity both with the somewhat quirky habits of the vehicle and the vagaries of the local traffic. He also displayed an unusual sticker on the sun visor in front of him which said "Swanky Lanky" which I took to be a reference to his local loyalties rather than his clearly diminutive size and dubious apparel.

'Ow do? Mr Manners is it?' the driver asked, 'you going t'golf?'

For a moment the accent gave me an uneasy feeling. It was as if I was back in Richmond, passing the living room door, hearing one of Ruth's peculiar television programmes. She says they keep her in touch with her roots. Odd really as her family come from Surrey.

'The golf? Indeed,' I said.

'Ay been reet busy at yon Oppen.'

'I imagine it has,' I said, somewhat pleased at my keen ear for dialect.

'Ay fowk been comin from all round.'

'I imagine they have.'

'Even got them politicians makin a reet how de do.'

A cold finger of apprehension seemed to stab at me. My hopes for a total escape from the smoke momentarily under threat. Of course, it would be natural for the local mayor or some such to attend, but with some foreboding I sensed that my driver was implying a somewhat higher level of dignitary. The transit van swept up to the main door of the club house.

'Politicians?' I asked

'Ay,' my driver said, 'that there Poppy Grimsdyke and some of her mates.'

Of all the bad luck. Poppy Grimsdyke; all those headlines that swirled around her; backbench bulldog; champion of the oppressed; storm trooper against the establishment. The one that appealed most to George, who, after all, was most in her firing line, was "The Grimsdyke Reaper" although I thought it was a little too laboured. For what it's worth my own favourite had always been "Poppy – Heroin of the North" until I discovered that missing "e" at the end of heroin was simply a typo; rather destroying the implied acuity of the headline.

However, more alarming right at that moment, as I stood indecisively in front of the club house, was that she had become Chair of the Social Exclusion committee, part of the Prime Minister's obligation to make the Civil Service and society even handed. We were, I was informed, aiming for statistical perfection—diversity by decimal point, inclusion by spreadsheet. You know the sort of thing; avoiding any type of discrimination other than the right sort; a utopian Civil Service where we would be 50.8 % female; 2.8% lesbian, gay, bisexual or transexual; 8.4% disabled, although how anyone can be 8.4% disabled, let alone 2.8% lesbian has always eluded me.

As I stood outside the building I thought about going back to the hotel, getting a message to Hugo to tell him I was indisposed, but Swanky Lanky had already headed off leaving an all too apparent trail of diesel smoke behind him. It wouldn't do to be spotted calling for a taxi and I didn't know the geography well enough to walk a back route to the hotel.

Hugo, it turned out, had set himself up on the upper floor of a rather imposing marquee, adjacent to the fifteenth fairway. A fact that Hugo was, for some reason, keen to point out. More importantly the whole affair exhibited a rather alarming swaying motion which gave it the effect of being at sea.

'Guy,' he said, 'wonderful to see you old boy. Such perfect timing. Lunch is about fifteen minutes away. Let me introduce you to some of my guests.'

I shook hands with the great and the good of Lancashire, the usual flurry of names exchanged and forgotten.

'One of the charming ladies here will get you a drink,' he gestured to two young women holding trays of champagne cocktails. I helped myself to a glass, taking a quick look round the place to see if I could see Poppy Grimsdyke lurking anywhere, but her ample frame was nowhere to be seen. It appeared that I was safe for the moment. Nevertheless, I kept an ear open for her laugh, a curious cross between a gulp and a wheeze that in anyone else might easily be mistaken for a medical condition. With any luck she was a guest in one of the other marquees. I began to relax.

Hugo was a good host. It was the same in college. Some people are designed to be good wine pourers as one of my early bosses observed, and Hugo was one such. Strange really as Hugo must have had precious little practice at the ancestral Baroncote Hall. More waited on than waiting was Hugo, as befitted the scion of a long-established mill owning dynasty. The family had, of course, long since traded cotton mills for cotton derivatives and an insurance empire.

I wandered round the table looking at the neatly inscribed place cards looking for my own; Ratcliffe, Butterworth, Bracewell, Entwistle; Thistlethwaite; Beaumont; Manners. As I reached my designated seat my blood ran cold. Whilst Hugo was seated to the right of me, the place card on my left, in elaborate gothic font, read Grimsdyke. With the eyes of Lancashire upon me I toyed with the idea of swapping the place cards but couldn't see how this could be achieved without raising considerable enquiry.

'Poppy Grimsdyke a guest of yours Hugo?' I asked, my voice just a little higher pitched than I would have wished.

'Remarkable lady,' Hugo said, with a glint in his eye, 'You know her of course?'

As I looked at him, with an abnormally smug look on his face; a face that deserved to be hit but couldn't be for obvious reasons, it occurred to me that there had to be more to this. I racked my brains for a common denominator. What on Earth could Poppy Grimsdyke have in common with Hugo? She might be a Northern MP, but Baroncote wasn't in her constituency. The idea of her taking an interest in the Beaumont businesses, other than to heckle from the side-lines, was inconceivable. There had to be something else, but before I could pin down the connection I heard a gulping wheezing laugh and turned to see Poppy bearing down on our table like the proverbial Assyrians sweeping down on a defenceless Jerusalem.

'Guy,' she said, checking her stride momentarily, 'how good to see you. Hugo told me you might be here and there's something I need to discuss with you.' She smiled. One of those smiles that can curdle eggs. 'You're such a difficult man to pin down in Whitehall.' She looked at the table and then back at me. 'So good to find a couple of hours when we won't be interrupted.'

From the corner of my eye, I saw Hugo turn away to talk to his other guests. The canvas walls of the marquee were billowing ominously, and the structure was swaying a little more noticeably. I grabbed another champagne cocktail from the hostess.

'I'll say grace, shall I?' Poppy said, without waiting for agreement. All ten of us stood holding onto the backs of our chairs for support as another gust of wind hit the marquee. Poppy, oblivious to the fact that the other tables were now seated and the food being served, gave us and God our marching orders. Then the connection came to me. Baroncote with its priest holes and chapel. Poppy and her campaign for Catholic women's ordination. Religion! Now I like a decent Christmas Carol as much as the next 49.8% man, but I've always found Religion rather disconcerting and somewhat prone to excessive facial hair, even occasionally in the 50.2% woman. My heart sank further. With a scraping of chairs, we sat down.

'I wanted to talk to you about social exclusion and cultural traditions,' Poppy said, attacking the plate of smoked salmon in front of her, 'I sent you a memo.'

'You did?'

She sighed before spearing a buttered slice of bread with her knife and transferring it to her side plate. 'I did.'

'Ah,' I said, 'well I'll most certainly look out for it when I get back to the office.'

'I'm rather afraid that some of our cultural traditions are enforcing social exclusion,' Poppy said.

'They are?'

I tried to think of any cultural traditions that weren't Judeo-Christian inspired. A picture of maypole dancers strangling people with their ribbons came briefly to mind.

'I'm particularly concerned about bonfire night.'

'You are?' I said, picturing chestnuts and foil wrapped potatoes baking on a fire, sparklers weaving patterns in the dark.

'I am.'

I turned to my right in the hope of diverting the conversation, but Hugo was ready to launch a pincer movement of his own.

'Real problem for us insurers dear boy,' he said, reaching over to fill my wine glass with a heavy looking Shiraz. 'Twenty-two per cent more thefts are reported on November the fifth.'

'But more importantly,' Poppy said, dismissing Hugo's intervention with a rather dry look, 'more importantly it is offensive to a significant part of the population.'

All those tedious history lessons came back to me; the accession of James I; Catesby and his conspiracy; the oppression of Catholics; barbaric executions.

'Do you really think that people worry about things that happened four hundred years ago?' I asked. 'I would have thought they just like watching a few fireworks.'

'Burning effigies of the Pope hardly constitutes a few fireworks,' Poppy said, glaring at me, another piece of buttered bread speared on her knife.

'And think of the injury risk,' Hugo said, 'important to have a moral dimension in the insurance business old boy.' Which was pretty rich I thought, since insurers were hardly renowned for ethical practices and Hugo himself came from a family that would, no doubt, have objected to planning consent for the building of Jerusalem amongst their dark satanic mills.

'Well,' I said, 'if the focus is about health and safety, then this is really a matter for the Department of Work and Pensions and the Health and Safety Executive. I'd be more than happy to pass the enquiry on.'

'Nonsense Guy, this is about the development, coordination and implementation of policy. That's your remit isn't it? You and George.'

And of course she was right. I spent a miserable two hours listening to the compelling case for banning bonfire night; the need for the cabinet office to research the position, with a foregone outcome, no doubt.

'After all,' Hugo said, as the dessert plates were mercifully being removed, 'we thought you had to be the right man for the job Guy,' he paused for effect, the smallest of smiles appearing at the corners of his mouth, 'has your name all over it.'

I could picture myself in the role of archetypal killjoy; the bureaucrat who banned bonfire night; Mandarin Launches Damp Squib; or a tabloid version – For Fawkes Sake Whatever Next. I could become the most unpopular man since Cromwell banned Christmas. What was more I could see all sorts of contributions from peculiar religious groups arguing different aspects; health and safety submissions; representations from the tourist industry. It might even get the civil liberties people going – the right to bear fireworks – and animal rights jumping on the band wagon. This was awful.

As Ratcliffe, Butterworth, Bracewell, Entwistle, and Thistlethwaite stumbled out of the marquee to watch the golf I headed in the opposite direction. The thought of a rematch at tea and dinner too much to bear. I left a message for Hugo at the reception desk to say I had been called away on urgent business, took a cab to the hotel, grabbed my unopened overnight bag and headed for the railway station.

I settled into my seat, trying to re-establish a sense of proportion, but however hard I tried, I could see no end to this. It would run and run. I'd gone to the Open to avoid the silly season. Turns out, the silly season had booked a seat next to mine. I wondered if Binky still had that guest house on the Isle of Wight.

A Fair Exchange

I know most people would think that working for
the Cabinet Office would be a good thing, being
right at the centre of things and all that. The trouble
is it means that you are always in the firing line for
latest great idea. In the old days a chap used to be
able to hide away in the historical section doing
some useful research, particularly after a good
lunch, but these days the whole place is more like
bomb alley with pretty much everything and
anything coming your way. The lunches aren't up
to much either. Years ago there used to be a rather
pleasant mess, served roast beef and spotted dick,
that kind of stuff. Now there are three metal and
glass cafeterias serving something they call
"healthy options." You know the sort of thing,
hummus and celery sticks. I avoid the place like the
plague.

It was one of those unavoidable last Fridays of
the month and I had to go in to put in my expenses.
Used to be so simple. A good old fashioned
expenses account. As long as it didn't amount to
more than a couple of thousand a month nobody
much cared. Had worked pretty well for a century
or more. Then came along the expenses scandal.
You remember, chaps charging for the odd duck
house, wheelbarrow repairs and manure. Personally,
I could never see the point of ducks, nasty noisy
creatures that keep you awake. I remember once,
Charlie Bairstow shooting one from the Magdalen
Bridge with a bow and arrow. Still, that's another

story. The fact is that paper wallahs these days like to see the whites of your eyes when you put the triplicate copies in. Even want receipts. Limits for this, limits for that; makes filling in the forms harder than Sudoku. Gives them a sense of power.

Anyway, I managed to couple the occasion with a rather pleasant lunch at the Wolseley. Thankfully, I wasn't paying, would have taken hours to redo the expenses forms, which I had safely sealed in a large envelope. It was good too to get away from the home front. Domestic harmony that morning had been thrown somewhat out of kilter owing to an unfortunate misinterpretation of something I said about Ruth's mother having the same birthday as Robert Mugabe. However, domestic concerns apart, I recall that the Filet de Boeuf was rather decent, and the company was quite good too. Oddly enough it was the very same Charlie Bairstow; useful sort of chap with a wine list, wanted to bend my ear about China of all things, and raised it just as we were finishing.

'It's going to be larger than the United States in the next couple of years,' he said, pouring out the last of a rather pleasant Haut-Médoc. Then sensing some apparent confusion on my part he added, 'GDP.'

'Ah,' I said.

'We've just submitted a report to government,' he said.

'Good for you,' I said enjoying the rather robust wine and wondering whether the paper-wallahs would mind if I put my expenses in on Monday.

'We rather think you should establish a government-linked centre for intense study and expertise on China. Set it up in the Cabinet Office, or the Foreign Office, something with a clear cross-Whitehall mandate.'

'Right,' I said although I seemed to remember that the Cabinet Secretary wasn't that keen on clarity. I wasn't that sure about "intense" either. Wasn't really George's thing as the younger generation would say.

'Well, the very best of luck,' I said.

'That's just it Guy.'

'What is?'

'It shouldn't be down to luck. It needs someone senior in the Cabinet Office to get behind it. I thought you might be just the man.'

Always been a bit other-worldly, Charlie. I remembered him at university. One of those chaps who got a first without breaking into a sweat, made the thing with the bow and arrow all the odder.

'Doesn't need much,' he said, as if sensing some reluctance on my part, 'just enough to make sure it doesn't get stuck on the wrong desk or buried in someone's in-tray for too long.'

'You really think it's *that* important?' I asked.

'Absolutely.'

Before I knew it I was promising to make sure the damn file had an easy passage, and Charlie was shaking my hand a shade too cheerfully for my liking.

It started to rain as I left the Wolseley, and I didn't have my trusty brolly. There's nothing more likely to disturb your average paper-wallah than a bundle of soggy receipts, so I popped into a likely looking shop to pick up an umbrella. I regretted instantly not having the foresight to bring my own, or to be near to James Smith to get a decent replacement. However, needs must. Ferreting through the plastic monstrosities with red hearts dotted here and there I alighted on a plain burgundy brolly with a discreet wooden handle. Comforting myself that this might double as a peace offering for Ruth, I paid and headed up Whitehall. The Cabinet Office was pretty empty, and I tried to slip past George's office to my own without him noticing.

I hung the ghastly brolly behind some coats on the umbrella stand, then, just as I passed his door, I heard George's voice boom out from deep within his office. 'Ah, Guy. Long time no see. Come in.'

I went in, closed the door, but held onto the handle in case the opportunity came for a quick exit.

'Just in to see the paper…'

'For heaven's sake don't call them paper-wallahs.' I could tell he wasn't in the best of moods. 'It's borderline racist. We're supposed to be a culturally diverse and vibrant organisation.'

'A what?' I asked.

'A culturally… Oh, never mind, look it up on the website.'

'The..?'

'Oh, don't be dense Guy,' he peered at me over those odd little spectacles he wears. Ones that might have been a gift from his days in the Russian embassy. 'I hope it wasn't too good a lunch.'

'No, no, just a quick catch up with Charlie Bairstow,' I said.

'Charlie Bairstow?' he reached up to adjust his spectacles. 'Ah yes, Magdalen Bridge and all that.'

'Indeed.'

'Bow and arrow.'

'That's the one.'

We both nodded and in that moment of shared experience I sensed an opportunity.

'You haven't come across a file on China have you?'

'China?' George shifted in his chair, tapped both sets of fingers on his desk, looked at his watch and then stood up. Not the usual tentative getting up, more a rush as he strode over toward me and put an arm round my shoulder. 'China, yes, yes indeed. Guy you could be just the man. Just in the nick of time.'

He reached past me to open the door and hurried me along the corridor; my envelope still clutched in my hand.

'We've got the Chinese Trade Minister, a Mrs Lee, arriving at Heathrow this afternoon. The Chancellor's doing a formal welcome this evening, but we need someone senior to meet her.' He turned to look at me. 'You know the drill, what the Americans call meet and greet, press the flesh, that sort of thing.' He looked again at his watch. 'Damned inconvenient that it's a Friday afternoon. Most of the chaps have got previous engagements.'

We positively barrelled down the corridor.

'I've got young Pennington trying to raise someone from the Foreign Office. He's already found an interpreter, a Dr Fang.'

'Pennington?'

'Keep up Guy. He's our new intern down from Cambridge. You remember, old Dicky Pennington's son.'

'Ah,' I said, as we burst into the main office, empty but for a pale looking youth holding onto a phone as if his life depended on it and a rather small thin Chinese gentleman, with a Fu Manchu style moustache and thin goatee beard staring inscrutably out of the window.

'Pennington,' George said, an unwarranted note of triumph in his voice, 'I've found your man. Couldn't ask for better. Guy's an old China hand. Aren't you Guy?' and before I could point out that it was nearly thirty years since I had had anything to do with China and couldn't stand the place, and nor could I see what on earth this had to do with the Cabinet Office anyway, he was gone.

'I er,' I said.

'Delighted to meet you Sir,' Pennington said, grabbing my hand with some alacrity, 'thought I was going to have to do this single-handed as it were. Massive responsibility and all that. Anyway, now you're here. What would you like me to do?'

The comforting afterglow of the Haut-Médoc was beginning to fade as I tried to think what needed to be done.

'The car's all ready and waiting Sir. The Minister lands at three-thirty.'

'We need gift,' Dr Fang said, the short beard wagging ominously as spoke.

'Right,' I said. 'Pennington, you dive out to the jewellers on the corner and get something.'

'What should I get?'

'Use your judgement,' I said.

'Nothing expensive,' Dr Fang said, 'mustn't think is bribe.'

'Quite,' I said, 'important to observe Chinese cultural sensitivities.' I paused to look at them. 'I'll just drop this off with the paper…er paper chaps and see you at the car in ten minutes.' I turned to go, then remembered just in time, 'make sure it's wrapped.'

I dived out of the room and down to the basement where the paper-wallahs had taken over part of the historical section and handed over my expenses. For once I elicited a grunt of acceptance rather than a list of remedial measures my forms would require in order to secure reimbursement. I popped up to the office to get the brolly and then headed down to the underground car park just in time to meet up with a breathless Pennington and Dr Fang, who looked even more like Fu Manchu in the gloom.

We crawled out toward Heathrow, Pennington in some agitation as the minutes ground out, Dr Fang occasionally stroking his thin beard, but otherwise staring impassively at the rain outside. As we neared the airport, it seemed to me that a little light conversation might lift the tension.

'So, what did you buy the Minister?' I asked Pennington.

Pennington brightened and reached into his pocket for a package, neatly wrapped in black tissue.

Dr Fang stared at the wrapping.

'It's black,' he said.

Even for me this seemed a remarkably straightforward observation, but looking at him, the colour draining from his face, coupled with some rather alarming beard tugging suggested there might be more to it.

'Indeed it is,' I said in what I hoped was an encouraging tone.

'Black is bad luck.'

'It is?' I asked, and some faint disturbing memory suggested that he might be right.

'In China it mean death or funeral,' he said.

'Well, we'll just take the tissue off,' I said, rather pleased that my capacity for logic hadn't wholly deserted me.

'I'm afraid it isn't quite that simple Sir,' Pennington said, proceeding to unwrap the gift as the car swept through the gates at Heathrow and headed onto the tarmac toward an obviously damp red carpet, and a long line of Chinese Embassy officials and cars.

The gift turned out to be a black-handled paperknife in a black box, cushioned on some rather tasteful, but nevertheless undoubtedly black, velvet. Any remaining colour in Dr Fang's face disappeared altogether and the beard tugging became dramatically faster, as if he were trying to pacify some terrified domestic cat.

'Well, it isn't exactly feminine is it Pennington,' I said, rather spectacularly missing the point as it turned out.

'This great insult,' Dr Fang struggled to get his words out, more a choke than a sentence, 'knife mean severing of relationship.'

'Ah,' I said, as Pennington and I stared at the shining and rather elegant paperknife, 'so, we are about to present the Chinese Minister of Trade with a welcome to Britain gift that says our meeting heralds a death and the relationship is being severed?'

Dr Fang nodded, his hand now clenched tight around the remains of his beard. The car drew up adjacent to the carpet; the droning noise of the slowing jet engines coming from a huge China Airlines Airbus A380. We spilled out onto the puddle strewn tarmac and bowed our way along the line of Chinese officials. The rain was steady, a fine spray making its way through the fabric of the brolly. We stood, huddled, as the steps were rolled into place and the doors opened. The rather striking Chinese Trade Minister stepped out for her first official visit to Britain.

Dr Fang stepped forward and introduced me and Pennington to Mrs Lee. I was rather surprised that the Minister spoke Cantonese. I waited for Fang to finish his rather inexact translation, my heart pounding. I burbled the usual phrases: delighted to

32

welcome…honoured guest…two great countries;
all the while thinking this could be it, the end of my
pension, cursing George for getting me into this in
the first place, and remembering how much I hated
China, however elegant their trade minister might
be.

Then I felt Pennington nudging the small gift
into my hand and oddly that bit of MacBeth started
to go round and round in my mind *is this a dagger I
see before me.*

All at once I had a brainwave, I palmed the
offending box into my pocket and with my very
best bow, handed my brolly to the Minister.

'I would like to extend this symbol of protection
as a gift to the Minister in the hope that the business
relations between our countries will flourish.'

She took the proffered brolly with a gracious
nod and smile as she waited for Dr Fang's
butchered and laboured translation.

'How thoughtful of you,' Dr Fang said,
translating the minster's words back to me, some of
the colour coming back into his face, 'and how
clever to know that red is a symbol of luck in
Chinese culture.'

I bowed again and explained that Pennington
and Fang would see her to her hotel and that I
hoped she enjoyed her stay. I watched them get into
the cars, thinking as they did that Mrs Lee looked
quite fetching under the burgundy brolly.

I made my way into the airport, absolutely drenched, but reflecting that it wasn't the first time that an England innings had been saved by rain. I felt for the paperknife. I wondered whether it would do as a peace offering for Ruth. Of course, if it did augur bad luck she might just stab me with it. A tangible severing of relations as it were. But Ruth wouldn't do anything rash. It would be bad form. On the other hand, I would have to fill in at least fifteen forms to have it taken off Pennington's expenses and get my money back. I decided to take my luck with Ruth.

A Close-Run Thing

The morning after my narrow escape with the
Chinese Trade Minister, there was a knock on the
bedroom door. A rather disconcerting rattle of
porcelain almost banished the last of a good night's
sleep. The door opened and a precariously balanced
teacup and saucer appeared followed by a smiling
Ruth. This was an occurrence about as likely as a
third eight rowing in the Oxford Cambridge boat
race. I could feel the blood draining from my face
as I rushed to sit up. I tried to encourage a few grey
cells to stir their stumps.

'Is the car alright?' I asked.

Ruth's lips twitched in an obvious determination
to purse themselves, but through some superhuman
effort they retained the remnants of a smile.

'Just bringing my husband a nice cup of tea,' she
said, placing the cup on the bedside table. She sat
on the edge of the bed. I looked at the tea. It was a
normal colour, uniform brown, no obvious lumps.

'Your mother's moving in,' I said.

'I want to talk to you,' she said, smoothing the
rumpled counterpane with the palm of her hand.
She looked at me. I resisted a sudden urge to pull
the bedclothes up a bit higher. I had the feeling that
this was either going to involve some outrageous
expense or one of those bizarre favours for one of
her bridge club friends. For some reason they

seemed to believe that working for the Cabinet Office gave me the power to reverse parking ticket fines, change planning consents, or reinstate weekly bin collections.

'It's about Joshua.'

'Joshua?'

'Your grandson,' she said, as if this was knowledge that I had somehow mislaid.

'Joshua,' I said again, in the hope of eliciting more useful information.

'Joshua,' she said, still smoothing the last of the wrinkles in the counterpane and inspecting a small blemish in the fabric. Apparently satisfied with the outcome of this scrutiny, she looked at me and clearly sensed some remaining confusion on my part. 'Oh, keep up Guy, it's half term the week after next.'

I tried to recall whether this was information that I was somehow expected to be aware of, but the cooling cup of tea suggested not.

'Jennifer has a problem with childcare.'

I looked at the remnants of Ruth's smile and back to the cup of tea. There was more to this than Ruth taking a few days out to go childminding.

'She and Trevor are going away to recharge their batteries,' Ruth said with a finality that brooked no opposition and ignored the flaw in any proposition that suggested that Trevor possessed a battery, or if he did, that he was ever likely to give it a chance to run down. 'We're going to take Joshua away.'

'We are?'

'Jennifer says that he loves MidParks.'

'MidParks?'

'Yes, you know, those activity places,' Ruth said, standing up. 'It'll do us some good too; get us some exercise. We'll get in a bit of cycling, take Joshua swimming that sort of thing. Anyway, I've booked an Executive Villa for us at the one in Wiltshire.'

Without waiting for any response, she picked up the cold cup of tea and left the room. By the time I got up, showered and shaved, she had already left for her Saturday morning at the charity shop; the weekly opportunity to spot someone from the bridge club searching through the clothes racks.

On Monday morning I popped into George's office to tell him that I would be taking the following week off.

'Oh, yes, where are you going Guy?' he asked with an obvious effort not to smile.

'Has Ruth been talking to you?' I asked.

He laughed. 'It's the joys of being a grand-father Guy. I'm sure Joshua will love it.'

'Have you actually been to this MidParks?'

'Can't say I have, old chap, but I hear the young people love it.'

My sense of dread for the forthcoming week was reinforced, by what was, in other ways, a passable lunch with Freddy Standish at the Savoy Grill. Freddy was one of those useful sorts of chaps who sat on the board of a dozen or so companies and was always keen to promote one or other of them. Wanted to bend my ear about government defence contracts.

'Not really our bailiwick old chap,' I said, when he asked mid-way through the main course, 'Ministry of Defence does the procurement.'

'Yes, yes I know that Guy,' Freddy said, getting a little too red in the face for comfort, 'but the Prime Minister must be concerned at the woeful state of the armed forces. First priority of government and all that.'

'Oh, I don't know,' I said, helping myself to another glass of the Montrachet, a millennium vintage bottle that elevated the rather bland Dover Sole. 'We didn't do that bad in Afghanistan did we? Speaking purely for myself you understand.'

'It's no laughing matter Guy. We only went into Afghanistan to toady up to the Americans. Gave them a good chance to laugh about the state of our ordnance. The country's going to the dogs,' he wagged his fork at me, 'and you know it.'

In an attempt to lighten the conversation, I asked. 'Freddy, do you know anything about MidParks?'

'We own it dear boy,' he said, now employing the fork more gainfully.

'What, your defence boys?'

'No, no, of course not. Do be sensible Guy. My venture capital friends own the sites. Ghastly places if you ask me, but solid cash generators.' The fork paused mid-air and then wagged at me again. 'David Miliband stayed there a while back.'

'David Miliband?'

'You know, Labour chappy, was Foreign Secretary for a while.'

'What was he doing there?'

'On holiday,' Freddy took a mouthful of fish before resuming, 'some ridiculous thing with his brother. You know; who can take the plebiest holiday; who is most in touch with the common man; that sort of thing.'

I found it hard to concentrate that afternoon, and it wasn't just the lingering uncertainty of the Dover Sole. This was worse than I thought. I'd never live it down. What was more I couldn't for the life of me understand what Ruth was doing encouraging the whole nonsense in the first place. After all it was enough of a set-back for a young chap to have a father like Trevor. Surely we should be encouraging Joshua to participate in more appropriate activities; the natural science museum; or even Madame Tussauds if absolutely necessary. Come to think of it there was plenty in London to satisfy even the most eclectic of young tastes. If the worst came to the worst we could go down to the house in Salcombe, introduce Joshua to a little bit of fishing.

I poured Ruth a gin and tonic as she settled down to watch some television dancing programme. 'Why don't we just show Joshua a bit of London? I'm sure he'd find it fascinating. We could go to the natural history museum; youngsters love dinosaurs. He'd have a whale of a time.'

Ruth looked at me, jaw clenched. 'It's what Joshua wants, Guy. Jennifer and Trevor took him to MidParks in the Spring, and he's been desperate to go back. Jennifer's told him that Granny and Granddad are going to take him, and he's really excited about the idea.'

This I could tell was not going to be easy, but desperate straits call for desperate measures. 'Why not go down to the house in Salcombe?' I asked, 'he'll love the beach. It's not as if we ever use the place that much.'

Ruth slammed her drink down on the coffee table with rather more force than normal and turned to me, arms crossed. 'You don't get it Guy, do you? This isn't about you. It's about your grandson. You don't think he wants to spend a week with his crusty old grandparents do you? But Jennifer has found something that he wants to do, something that he is happy to do with us.' She unfolded her arms and started pointing a finger at me. 'He's four. He is not going to spend a week mouldering in museums or sitting watching you murder some poor fish in Devon. He's going to have a week he enjoys.' The finger came closer. 'I don't particularly want to go, you don't want to go, but come what may Guy, we are going to make sure he has a good time.' She sank back in the sofa. 'Now go away I'm going to watch Strictly It Takes Two.' Whatever that was.

There was no point in pursuing the matter, but the arrival of the brochures on the Wednesday prompted me to have one last go.

'Have you read these?' I asked politely over the breakfast table.

'Read what?' Ruth asked from behind the pages of the Daily Mail.

'These brochures.' There was no answer, so I read out an extract from one of them.

Your Guide to Swimming Safely: Please encourage children to use the toilet before swimming and ensure that babies wear a swim nappy. You must not enter the water if you have suffered from a gastro-intestinal upset involving diarrhoea within the past forty-eight hours.

'Are you sure this is the sort of place we should be taking Joshua?' I asked, hoping to appeal to Ruth's innate fear of bacteria.

Ruth straightened the pages of the newspaper with a brief, determined flick of her wrists, but did not emerge from behind the tabloid pages. I cleared my throat.

'Not another word Guy,' Ruth said, emphasising each word. I could hear a sucking of teeth that suggested a cessation of any further discussion on the matter. I tucked the brochures in my briefcase, slipped out, and for the want of anything better to do, went to the office.

I managed to find some useful research that required my presence in the historical section. I thought I might head off to the club for lunch in the absence of anything else and was just heading down the corridor when I heard a voice calling after me.

'Sir! Sir!'

I turned and saw young Pennington hurrying toward me. For a second I thought he might be looking to involve me further with Mrs Lee and started to look at my watch in a feeble attempt to suggest that I might be on my way to a meeting.

'Sir,' Pennington said, somewhat out of breath as he caught up with me. 'I just wanted to say thank you for all your help on Friday. Dug me out of a frightful hole. I know the Foreign Office and the Business Department are enormously grateful. Seems it was a terrible misunderstanding. Whole thing fell between a couple of stools.'

'Good, good,' I said, 'well, glad it all worked out alright.'

'Would you care for a sandwich or something?' Pennington asked, and then glancing at my watch, 'if you're not busy that is.'

Pennington's idea of a sandwich was a healthy option in the cafeteria. As I stared at the menu, I could feel a sense of gloom wash over me. It wasn't as if there was a limited choice; the notorious hummus and celery sticks were still available, as were: artichoke parcels and pasta: Latvian potato bake: spinach lasagne: and other concoctions too ghastly to mention. Nothing remotely edible for a main course and after much deliberation I plumped for Fabulous Falafel, more out of curiosity for the contrived alliteration than anything else, and using the same rationale opted for a Super Smoothie as a drink.

'Wonderful menu here Sir, isn't it?' Pennington smiled, 'makes all the difference having good food. It is so easy to eat badly when you're working don't you agree?'

I nodded, too depressed to endorse this burst of youthful and entirely misplaced enthusiasm. There are times I fear for the future of the Country.

While we waited for Pennington's Black Bean Burger and ginger tea, I tried to summon up some interest in proceedings. 'So, how is Dicky these days?' I asked, remembering Pennington's father, the one-time Ambassador for far flung places and scourge of Whitehall, with his wonderful handlebar moustache and alarming eye-patch.

'Couldn't be better, thank you Sir. He and mother retired up to Scotland. Small estate in Galloway. He enjoys the shooting.'

The idea of Dicky galumphing round the countryside, shooting half-blind, no doubt scaring the natives to death, cheered me up a little and inspired me to probe young Pennington a bit further.

'So, what do you do for leisure er…'

'Simon, Sir.'

'Simon?' I asked.

'Anything outdoors. You know; triathlons; parascending; that sort of thing.'

'Have you ever been to MidParks?' I asked.

He laughed. 'It used to be a birthday treat when my father was posted in Belgium. Great place up by the Dutch border. Loved the tree-trekking.'

'Tree-trekking?' I asked, picturing a pleasant nature walk through attractive woodlands, holding my young grandson's hand and explaining the different varieties of tree. For the first time I could picture us sharing time together. The calm peaceful enjoyment of the natural world.

'It's an aerial course of ropes, walkways and zipwires strung between the trees. It's an awesome experience.'

I'm not sure which was the greatest shock; the idea of my trying to emulate Tarzan in some artificial theme park; or the arrival of the Fabulous Falafel; five brown balls of indeterminate and dubious substance sitting uncomfortably on a bed of green leaves. It all had a kind of unpleasant rural aspect to it. Even the aroma had a suggestion of meadows and dairy herds that managed to kill any remaining appetite that I had. I dissected one of the balls to discover a crumbly substance that had a disturbingly green hue to it. I pushed it around my plate.

'Lovely,' Pennington said, munching away manfully at his Black Bean burger. Then looking out of the window he went on. 'Great place MidParks. They light up the trees at night in different colours you know.' I must have appeared a little disconcerted as he added, 'pink, blue, green, that sort of thing.'

Somehow I managed to make it appear as if I had eaten some of the food and insisted on paying. As I slumped away from the cafeteria. I bumped into George, who looked a bit surprised to see me in the vicinity.

'Are you alright Guy? You look a bit pale? There was that familiar look he had that suggested he knew something I didn't.

'Fine, fine,' I said.

'I suspect fresh air, and exercise is just what you need.' He smiled and made to move away than paused. 'By the way, Ruth called. Spoke to me as you were away from your desk. Seems young Joshua has gone down with hand, foot and mouth disease. Won't be able to go to MidParks with you next week.' He looked at me. 'Shame isn't it. These opportunities don't come round that often do they?'

The Panama Hat

On the third day of the third test at Lords I was a guest at the match against South Africa, quite a nail-biter. A hot day, wall to wall sunshine and I'd come in my blazer, tie and Panama hat, not an MCC one, I've never been a member, but decent enough with a blue ribbon, a hat that I'm fond of. Lords are sticklers for dress code; they've even put up pictures of what is acceptable on their website. It was Lords that introduced me to the term 'toe cleavage', showing too much toe, especially female toe, is overly disturbing for the members. A hat is acceptable as long as it isn't too large, essential during hot weather, but a nuisance in the pavilion. During the lunch and tea breaks it never seems right to put it under your seat; inconvenient to check it into the cloakroom for a short time; you can't wear it, and so when I get invited I've found a small shelf where some members, faced with the same problem, put theirs. An acceptable solution, mine was the only blue-ribboned Panama and no one objected to its being there.

That Saturday was no different to my other visits to Lords. The ground was packed; the weather glorious; the game poised. The Olympics were over, and people wanted to hold on to the sporting fervour of an amazing summer. Not that cricket is associated with fervour, but there was a good atmosphere. The pavilion seemed busy, but then it often was. I regretted that I wasn't going to be able to stay for the final session. Ruth's mother was with us for the weekend, and I'd only been allowed to go at all on the promise of dinner.

I said my thank-yous and farewells after the tea break, walked to St John's Wood tube station, made the two changes to get onto the district line that would take me home, and settled back for the long tube ride. It was sweltering and I used the hat to fan a bit of air across my face. Then I noticed that it wasn't my hat. It looked the same, same size, same straw, same weave, even the same blue ribbon, but the label inside, the one that said it was made in Ecuador, a genuine Panama hat, was missing. I wondered whether the label had been torn out or tucked inside the inner band, but it wasn't there. I felt a twinge of annoyance. I had picked up the wrong hat. Someone had picked up mine. It wasn't an expensive one, it cost about £100, but I liked it, the only one I'd ever had that felt comfortable and didn't make me look stupid. I couldn't see how I was going to get it back. I should have put my name in it or made it more distinctive. I looked at the poor substitute I held in my hands to see if there were any identifying marks. Perhaps if I could find its owner I could get my beloved hat back. There was nothing obvious to give me a clue, but as I ran my finger inside the blue ribbon I found a small scrap of paper. I pulled it out, trying to make sure I didn't tear it or damage the ribbon. The paper had been torn from a small notebook, and when I opened it out, wonder of wonders, a mobile phone number. Thank heavens, I thought, that the other chap had been more sensible than me.

There was no signal on the tube, but I called the number as soon as I got into the station at Richmond. To my annoyance there was no answer or introductory message, but I reasoned that the chap was still watching the last few overs, ignorant of the fact that he was wearing my hat. I left a polite message explaining the mistake, leaving my number and asking if he wouldn't mind getting in touch at his convenience.

Back home, Ruth and her mother were already trying on their glad rags, so there was no choice but to get changed and take them out to a rather nice Italian I knew. Ruth's mother liked steak with pizzaiola sauce; a great way to earn back the brownie points lost through my absence at the cricket. It was a successful evening.

In the morning there was no message for me on the mobile and over breakfast, before her mother got up, I decided to risk reawakening Ruth's disapproval of my absence the previous day by recounting the tragedy of my hat.

'I don't know what you're worrying about Guy. That hat is years old. If you must waste your time at the cricket, why don't you get a new one?' She turned a page of the Daily Mail.

'But I like that hat. In fact, it's the only one that I've ever liked.'

She lowered the paper and peered at me over the top of her reading glasses.

'Well, it seems like a lot of fuss over nothing to me.'

'I'm going to call this chap again after breakfast. It may just be that he stayed on after the match or something and didn't get my message.'

'Well dear,' she said, 'I'm sure you know best, but it sounds like a bit of a wild goose chase to me.' The Daily Mail was raised again, and I knew the conversation was over.

I called from the landline and a rather sleepy female voice answered.

'Ah, sorry to disturb you. My name's Guy Manners. I left a message about my Panama. I found your number in a hat I picked up by mistake and wondered if perhaps it was your husband's? I'd be more than happy to come round to pick it up if you have it.'

'Panama? Oh yes, you leave message. You want come round?'

I couldn't quite understand what she was saying, her accent was very thick, vaguely Chinese, and I wondered if she was perhaps the housekeeper.

'Do you have my Panama? If so, I can come round to collect it.'

'Oh yes, Panama, have Panama. It fifty pounds. Can see you ten.'

Incensed at the thought that she was asking for money for an old hat, I tried to laugh it off. 'Well,

I'm sure you know best. I'm afraid my Panama has no real value, but I will bring you yours, or rather your husband's.'

'I see you ten.'

The address was in Acton. I had to ask twice to make sure I got it right and then booked a taxi to take me there. I was a bit thoughtful, couldn't picture the sort of chap who would live in Acton and go to Lords, but London is an odd place these days, full of all sorts and I was pleased to think that I was going to get my trusty Panama back.

I was outside the building just before ten o'clock, holding the impostor Panama and the scribbled note of the address. I asked the taxi driver to wait, saying I wouldn't be long. He gave me a doubtful 'Alright Guv' in response, and I went up the path of an imposing, dilapidated, Victorian, brick built, three storey, semi-detached house. I checked the address and pressed the button for Flat 4a. The main door opened, and I went up the stairs, the old-fashioned sort with a white painted banister and worn red carpet. There was a sweet and unpleasant smell I couldn't quite place, mingling with the scent of cheap perfume. I could hear music and muffled voices coming from several flats and began to regret my decision to come, but victory was so close at hand that it seemed ridiculous not to see the thing through.

Flat 4a was on the second floor. A nondescript white painted door with a Yale lock, security peep hole and an entry buzzer set in the wall which I pushed. I sensed movement behind the door which then opened. I stepped inside. It was an appalling mistake. The young lady was under-dressed in the most inappropriate garb.

'I have Panama,' she said pointing to a box of cigars and an ashtray on the coffee table. 'You want now or later?'

'I'm afraid there's been the most frightful mistake.' I said, clutching the impostor Panama in front of me. 'I thought you had my hat you see.'

She looked confused, but further explanation proved impossible as a loud banging noise erupted from the stairwell outside, followed by the sound of heavy feet running up the stairs, splintering wood and shouting. The young lady's eyes opened wide, and she bolted for the window and an uncertain-looking fire escape. As she was struggling with the sash window a policeman burst into the room and grabbed me by the arm, followed by a woman police officer who took control of the young lady.

The next part is too embarrassing to relate. The police were disinclined to believe my story about the hat and put me in the back of a police van with a couple of other chaps, one of whom was sporting a nasty bruise under his eye.

At the police station I called my lawyer, Gerald. I could tell he wasn't pleased to have his Sunday interrupted, but he agreed to come and sort things out. It was an age until he came. I don't know if you've ever been inside a police cell. The boys in blue do their best to keep them clean, but the residual smells, overlaid with disinfectant, are most off-putting. When Gerald arrived, the police took me through to an interview room where I told him my story.

'And you expect me to run with that?' he asked when I finished.

'What do you mean?'

'Well, it's a bit thin old boy. You might do better admitting it.'

'Admit what?' I began to feel hot and cold, and my mouth was dry. 'I've never, I mean you can't possibly believe...you actually think I would...?'

'Listen Guy, the police will agree bail you, so you'll be out of here in an hour or so whatever you decide to do. I understand that there is only limited evidence that you have committed an offence with this er.' He looked down at his notes,' Vanida Tongproh. You have no criminal record, so I may be able to get them to agree to a simple caution.' He stared at me for longer than I thought was necessary and then added, 'In which case you can avoid all the publicity of a trial.'

'But what happened to innocent until proven guilty?' I asked. 'I've told the truth. Why should I admit to something I haven't done?'

'Well, let's go over the facts.' He started counting them off on his fingers. 'You made an appointment to meet a prostitute.'

I argued, but he held up his hand.

'Let me finish. You made an appointment to meet a prostitute; according to her you agreed terms; you were arrested in her room; and you have no satisfactory explanation to account for your presence there. In your favour you were dressed; no money had changed hands; and I think the taxi driver may corroborate the fact that you had only just arrived.' He paused. 'If it goes to trial you'll lose. They're cracking down on this sort of thing and heaven only knows what Miss Tongproh may come up with in due course. It may be that she was not undertaking this er... role voluntarily, in which case you are party to something far worse. They'll want to make an example of you.' He paused again. 'Imagine how it'll look in the press. Forty-eight-year-old senior civil servant in sex scandal. They'll have a field day. You might even lose your job, and what about Ruth?'

I swallowed, 'This is terrible. What am I going to tell Ruth?'

'Well, if you are going to defend this, then you could tell her your version of the truth and see what happens. If you take the caution it's up to you to decide. The caution remains on your file for a period and has no other real consequence.'

I closed my eyes. This was unfair, and yet I had been stupid. I should have realised something was odd when I spoke to the wretched woman on the phone, but I'd been fixated on the possibility of getting my hat back. The thought of trying to explain it to Ruth was inconceivable. She would never understand.

'I don't need to tell anyone about this?' I asked.

'No, you just have to make an admission of guilt.'

'It seems wrong.'

'Well, it's up to you Guy. Look, I'll give you a few minutes to think it over while I see if I can line it up with the duty Sergeant.'

He stood up, scraping the plastic chair along the lino, and signalled to the police officer outside to be let out. I sat there alone, my head in my hands. I thought about those American plea-bargaining cases you read in the paper, British businessmen forced to admit guilt in order to avoid lengthy sentences. There was always a sneaking feeling that they were guilty. People would think the same of me if they found out, although Gerald seemed confident that they wouldn't, and, damn it, I wasn't guilty.

I had no real choice. Right is right and all that, and I can't say I felt comfortable swearing an admission to something I hadn't done, but I couldn't risk losing everything. Ruth would never forgive me, and it would have been a travesty to lose my job with my pension in sight and all that. I lied on oath, claimed I was one of those chaps who did that sort of thing and signed the form. It was wonderful to be out of the police station. Gerald got a cab to take me home and I have never been so relieved.

'Find your hat then Guy?' asked Ruth as I got in.

'No, you were right dear, it was a wild goose chase.'

'Well, what a waste of a morning, and you are only just back in time for lunch.'

'I think you were right dear, I'll just buy myself a new Panama.'

I watched the smile on her face, the one that says, 'I always know best'. Just that once it was hard to disagree.

The Drive for Efficiency

'The PM's concerned about public sector waste, Guy.' George had one of his serious looks. The one that said he didn't believe in what he was saying but was going to see it through anyway. 'He wants £100 million in savings. Even civil service cuts are on the table.'

'Ah,' I said thinking of the usual focus on all the essential entertainment we were obliged to do at Glyndebourne, Henley, or heaven forbid, Lords.

'Quite,' said George, reading my mind. 'We need to approach this from a different angle,' he said, indicating that I should take a seat, which I did.

'We couldn't say that we don't have a budget for it – went in the last spending review. Be a bit costly to reinstate it. That sort of thing?'

George moved his mouth from side to side, like a man trying to extract the last drop from a lemon sherbet.

'No,' he said eventually. 'Good idea but won't wash. PM's got a real bee in his bonnet wants to create some headroom in the overall budget.'

'What for?' I asked.

'Some pet project.' George coughed. The usual sign that he knew what it was but was sworn to secrecy and didn't approve. 'He wants a war chest, something high-level and politically sensitive.'

It was not a turn of phrase George often used, so it had to be serious. 'Ah,' I said again, trying to think of any angles we hadn't tried before. 'Perhaps the biggest spenders…?' I ventured.

'Hm,' George said. 'Can't do health. Sacred cow and all that.'

'Are we allowed to say sacred cow?' I asked, thinking of the diversity training we'd just had, or had it been the inclusivity training or maybe the cultural sensitivity training? I couldn't remember which one was which.

George looked at me but couldn't quite bring himself to say what I knew he wanted to say.

'Institutional taboo,' he said instead.

I wasn't sure that "taboo" didn't feature somewhere, but I didn't press the point. 'Education?'

'Sacred…taboo,' George said with a look that dared me to correct him.

We headed down the list of spending departments.

'Police?' I said getting to the seventh on the list and the Home Office budget.

'Have we reviewed them before?' George asked.

'Not that I can recall.'

'Hm,' George said, and I knew that he was thinking about the speeding fine he collected the previous week doing forty along the West Way. Really annoyed according to Ruth who swore me to secrecy. Told Ruth it was a poor show, he was supposed to set an example that sort of thing, weighed on his mind apparently and he'd sworn that he wasn't a fraction over the speed limit, dodgy camera and all that.

'Police it is,' he said with a smile. 'Well done Guy. I'd like your report in two weeks.'

'Me?' I said, thinking of the opprobrium likely to be heading my way from the boys in blue, or is it girls, or is it…what is it? But by the time I got through the quagmire of diversity, inclusivity, or decolonisation, it was too late. I'd failed to get my defence in quick enough.

'That's settled then,' George said with, I have to say, something of a triumphant glow that I felt was unwarranted.

As I left his office I felt that familiar slough of despond descend upon me. Spending reviews of any description are like the bureaucratic equivalent of garlic to a vampire. A notion, so institutionally radioactive, that even mentioning it in meetings causes spontaneous coughing, and a mysterious outbreak of diary conflicts.

I wondered whether I could call in sick for the next fortnight, but that would have been a bad show, and I felt that I couldn't leave George in a bind on this one. Perhaps I could put out feelers, see if I could find out what the PM wanted the money for, cut off the problem at the root as it were. I put in a call to Charlie Hobson at the Daily Insult and in his absence left a message. If anyone knew what was happening at the top of government I reasoned it would be Charlie.

In the meantime, I needed someone young and bright to act as a foil. Avoiding lunchtime and the risk of falafel in the cafeteria—once was enough—I went in search of young Pennington.

With some relief I found him, not in the canteen, but in the large office that was designated for hot-desking, a concept I have never really been able to grasp, particularly as most of the younger staff have taken to working from home, a concept of which I can only say that I wished it had existed when I was their age.

'Hello, Sir,' Pennington said as he saw me approach.

'Ah, Pennington,' I said. 'Just the chap.'

'Simon, sir.'

'Of course, of course. How's Dicky these days?'

'Very well, Sir, thank you. I took the liberty of mentioning that I had had the honour of working with you.'

'Ah,' I said, thinking of the various interactions I had with young Pennington's father—most of which would be better left in the diplomatic shadows.

'Said to mention Lilongwe to you. Said he had very fond memories.'

'That was good of him,' I said, recalling the horrified expressions on the faces of the good ladies of Malawi as Dicky attempted, in Swahili, to commend the strengthening of ties between our two great nations—only to deliver something altogether more suggestive. Mind you I was never entirely convinced it was a mistake—despite his protests. With Dicky, you could never be sure. Especially not beneath that eye patch. Anyway, keen to move away from more disturbing events I asked, 'What are you up to at the moment Pen…Simon?'

Pennington glanced at his laptop. 'The PM asked me to provide a briefing on Youth Engagement.'

'Promoting marriage?' I asked, thinking of the PM's latest crusade for traditional values.

Pennington looked confused and glanced again at his laptop. 'Well, I had rather assumed that it was about TikTok, Instagram that sort of thing.'

'I'm sure you're right,' I said trying a smile to demonstrate that I had caught up with these new-fangled ideas. 'Anyway, the PM has a new directive that I need your help with.'

'Wonderful,' Pennington said, standing straighter and with that genuine enthusiasm of youth that the Civil Service takes at least twelve months to dispel.

'The PM is initiating a drive against waste.'

'Well, I've always thought…'

'Yes, quite,' I said, hoping to convey that some things are best unsaid. 'Anyway, we have to prepare an overview of waste in the Police service.'

Pennington's eyes were even brighter than before, bursting with an enthusiasm that seemed so misplaced that I wondered whether a career in the civil service was entirely suited to him.

'I have a cousin who works in the Home Office internal audit, and he says…'

'Do you really?' How wonderful,' I said, wondering whether I had opened a Pandora's, or should I say Pennington's, box. I racked my brains for a way to divert this potential black hole from swallowing our rather pleasant little galaxy and it occurred to me that Ruth also had a cousin in the Metropolitan Police. Something to do with strategic partnerships. The name came to me, Monty Featherstone. Thin looking chap with a prominent Adam's apple, uncontrollable eyebrows and an obsession with geraniums.

'I've arranged a meeting with the Commissioner in charge of strategic partnerships to start with.' Well, it would be true as soon as I pinned Monty down, probably at Freemason's Hall, if I recalled correctly.

'But aren't strategic partnerships more outward-looking than inward-looking?' Pennington looked distinctly confused.

'Always good to get a helicopter view to start with,' I said, logging away the thought that helicopters didn't seem to fall foul of anything in the way of cultural sensitivity.

An hour later and the taxi pulled up outside Freemason's Hall.

'Shouldn't we have taken the tube?' Pennington asked. 'I mean it's much cheaper and if we're supposed to be reviewing waste, shouldn't we set an example for Mr Featherstone?'

I could have said that I doubted very much that it was an example Mr Featherstone would have any intention of following, but it would have taken too long. 'Security considerations,' I said sensing a brief acceptance from young Pennington and diving inside before he could mount any further challenge.

'Guy!' a voice called from the gloom. 'How wonderful to see you. How's Ruth?'

'Monty. It's been a long time. Ruth sends her best, hopes the geraniums are thriving.'

Monty held out his hand and gave me one of those handshakes. The one that says "I'm a Worshipful Master or Deputy Grand Warden" or something like that. It's never appealed to me, never could get my mind round those leather aprons and always worried about getting stabbed with one of those trowels.

'Won first prize in the Battersea flower show.' Monty's eyebrows were doing a sort of uncoordinated war dance.

'Splendid,' I said.

'And the Chelsea Physic Garden asked me to lecture on scented-leaf geraniums and their history.'

'Quite an honour, I'm sure.'

'Did Ruth tell you I'm writing a book on Pelargoniums?'

'I can't think of anyone better qualified.' I paused. 'Monty, sorry to trouble you, but we've come to pick your brains about the police.' I gestured to Pennington. 'This is Pen…Simon Pennington. Old Dicky's son. You remember Dicky?'

Monty reached up towards his eye but stopped himself. The allusion to Dicky's eye patch was obvious.

'Quite,' I said.

'Knew your father very well,' Monty said as he shook Pennington's hand. 'Not on the square then?' Monty turned a puzzled glance at me.

'I don't believe so,' I said, although why he would automatically assume Pennington was a Mason eluded me for a second. Then it came to me that Old Dicky must have been a member. That explained a lot.

'Anyway,' Monty said, 'Come on through. We have the café pretty much to ourselves this afternoon.'

The café was imposing in that heavy art-deco way, and we sat at a table while Monty ventured up to the counter to procure coffee.

'What is it?' Pennington asked, looking in awe at the coffee and cream ceilings and columns and rather sparse burgundy furniture.

'How do you mean?' I asked.

'Is it safe?'

I looked at Pennington. It was either the most naïve or most wise question that I think had ever been posed of me and for a second I couldn't decide which. But given the rather wide-eyed gape that Pennington was displaying I plumped for naïve.

'It's the Grand Lodge,' I said.

Pennington looked confused.

'Your father's never talked about it?' I asked, reflecting on Monty's surprise that Pennington junior was not a member of his hallowed institution.

Pennington shook his head.

'Well, perhaps best to ask him about it next time you see him. For the meantime audi, vide, tace,' I said, echoing the masons' rather didactic motto. Then in the face of further incomprehension. 'Hear, see, be silent.'

Monty returned with the coffees, rather spectacular cappuccinos with the square and compass in chocolate adorning the froth.

'So, what can I do for you Guy? Something about the police? Not more problems with our brothers in Acton, I hope?' He smiled and his eyebrows positively glided up his forehead.

'Thank you for reminding me, Monty. That was years ago. No, this is an altogether more serious matter. The PM is looking to review waste in the police service.'

Monty choked on his cappuccino, blowing the square and compass into more of a triangle and needle. 'You can't be serious Guy?' He said once the coughing stopped.

'Deadly,' I said.

'But why us? I mean we're pared to the bone as it is. Open our cupboard and you'll find it bare. The days of driving in Jaguars has long gone you know. Have to make do with those German jalopies.'

I wasn't sure that being chauffeured in a BMW was worse than being chauffeured in a Jaguar, but I refrained from making the point. In any event I could see that Monty was disturbed, even his eyebrows had a hangdog expression.

'Who knows the vagaries of the Prime Ministerial searchlight,' I said. 'But it has decided to alight on you.'

'But you must stop it, Guy, get it to move on to more fertile ground, lower hanging fruit, that sort of thing. Dammit you know, Guy, I've given my life to this service. It's not perfect, but it matters.'

'Out of my hands, dear boy,' I said, ignoring the mixed metaphor. 'Besides, there must be some dark corners that the Prime Minister's searchlight can safely be shone into.'

'Ah,' Monty said, catching my drift. 'Ah, I see what you mean.' His eyebrows were a forest of concentration. 'I think you might want to take a look at the Royal Parks Police. Always have thought that a well upholstered operation.'

I looked at Monty for a moment. It was an inspired suggestion. We could look at the waste of money on Royal Parks and protection, identify oodles of savings, safe in the knowledge that it would all be torpedoed in the PM's weekly meeting with the King. It was such a good idea that I couldn't understand why I hadn't come up with it myself.

'Excellent, Monty. I knew you were the man to talk to.'

Monty positively beamed and his Adam's apple bobbed up and down as if bowing. 'You must come to the rugby, Guy. Got the force to sponsor the varsity match at Twickenham. Best seats and all that, champagne picnic in the car park. Do bring Ruth.'

'Most kind of you Monty. I'm not sure that rugby is Ruth's thing, but I will most certainly mention it.'

We parted company, Monty clearly keen to enlist young Pennington into the ranks of the leather frock brigade and I whisked him away to a taxi as Monty pressed the promise of geraniums in both our directions.

'How did we save on waste?' Pennington asked.

'We didn't,' I said. I do wonder whether the country will be in safe hands when the Penningtons of this world take over. 'We have identified a rich seam of potential savings.'

'But aren't the Royal Parks important?' Pennington asked.

'Absolutely vital,' I said, anticipating George's pleasure at the elegant solution.

Ruth was waiting for me when I got home. I could sense in her frown that something was more amiss than usual. She had that Disraeli pose, the folded arms and pursed lips. Buoyed by my good humour I could hear the great man say, "You can tell the strength of the nation by the women behind its men," although the idea of Ruth behind me was not altogether comfortable, nor on reflection could Disraeli have had the benefit of Civil Service equality training for that matter.

'Have you been bullying Monty?' She asked.

'Bullying, my angel, does not feature in the civil service lexicon. It is a sine qua non…'

'Don't get all lyrical with me Guy. It sounds pompous and it doesn't suit you. I want to know why you were bullying Monty.'

'Who says I was bullying Monty?'

'Monica. Says Monty is most upset, won't come out of the greenhouse.'

'Well, I don't know why he should be upset. Together we have struck a blow for liberty and justice…'

'Guy!' The arms were unfolded, always an uncomfortable moment that heralds either a full-blown review of my shortcomings or a week of uncomfortable silence, or in extreme cases, both. But this particular charge did seem unjust.

'Well, if he is so upset, why did he invite us to the Varsity match?'

'Sometimes I despair, Guy. Monty's a tender soul and you should remember who your friends are.'

So saying, she swept from the room and as she did I recalled another Disraeli quote "It is easier to be critical than be correct" – indeed he might well have had Ruth in mind when he coined the phrase.

I was, however, genuinely perplexed by Monty's distress, and I considered giving him a call, but there was nothing in the meeting we had that could have given rise to any concern and the solution we arrived at was as elegant as they come. I decided to leave it.

When I arrived at the office the next morning I was summoned by George, a meeting I was looking forward to, given the success of the previous day.

'What are you playing at?' George asked as I entered.

Taken aback by this opening gambit I could only stand and stare.

'What the devil is this?' George threw a thick report across the table. It had the ghastly look of something thorough. George wafted a hand at it as if dispersing an unpleasant smell. 'I thought I made it clear that I wanted a review, not an assassination.'

'We did, I mean I did. I mean I thought the Royal Parks police…'

'It's your mess, Guy. Take that damn thing away and find a way to deal with it. Otherwise, it will be your head that's the first on the chopping block.'

I scrabbled for the report that had to be four hundred pages long and retreated to the safety of the archives, finding a corner where I could study it undisturbed.

As I read the pages I began to feel faint. It had to be what distressed Monty so much, and I wasn't surprised. It was a catalogue of ineptitude and waste in the police service. I began to read it with a morbid fascination.

*In February, Police conducted a controlled explosion on a suspicious vehicle parked outside *** station—later discovered to have been left there by their own colleagues. The incident, which cost approximately £2,000 and involved Ministry of Defence personnel, ammunition, and fuel, was attributed to an "internal communications error."*

In one case, a police station refurbishment contract included a perimeter fence quoted at £68,000—later estimated by a local contractor to be achievable for under £3,000. The inflated cost was attributed to a combination of consultancy input, stakeholder engagement, and "exclusion sensitivity" assessments, which appear to have involved a series of workshops on fence symbolism and its impact on community cohesion.

A resident has received over forty mistaken police visits in eighteen months due to a persistent address confusion between Duncton Road and

I felt sick. I could see the police budget cuts coming and on the back of them I would be loathed by the police for eternity. It would never be safe to drive the car again.

I scrambled to find the author of this death wish. It was some Home Office Internal Auditor, one of those dreadful whistleblowers one hears about but hopes never to meet. And then it dawned on me, Pennington's cousin, the one he was keen to introduce. What had I done? I sat and stared at the rows of files, each one a buried bomb safely defused in this precious vault like so many vampires each with a stake through its heart, never to be bothered again by the light of day. But what was I going to do? I couldn't just forget the report. It wouldn't just die unaided. It had enough oxygen to give it life. I had to find a way to strangle it before it grew too big.

I headed back to my office, the beastly report under my arm. For once I was completely at a loss. I threw the blasted thing on the desk and sat down. I might as well resign, try to distance myself from the whole ghastly affair. I might still preserve my pension after all. I was mulling over the complete absence of options when I spotted a note saying that Charlie Hobson had returned my call.

'Charlie,' I said, as I managed to get through to him.

'Guy, dear boy. Do you know I had an inkling that you might call?'

'Oh yes, why's that?'

'Little birdie told me that the PM is out for some immediate cuts.'

'I couldn't possibly comment, Charlie.'

'I think you can, Guy, because I may just have some information you might want. The same little birdie told me the PM's been sniffing around the constitutional cellar again. Wants to uncork something vintage.'

How Charlie knew these things I never found out. It was as if he had managed to bug the whole of Whitehall, but the boffins always assured me that it wasn't possible.

'Club in thirty?' I said.

'Perfect.'

I'm sure that the Club continues to retain its atmosphere of studied calm, not even ruffled by the recent decision to provide copies of the Daily Express as well as the Telegraph, Times and Mail, but in my agitation at the time, the balming effect of the place was lost on me.

Charlie was already ensconced in the library, flicking through the pages of the Express.

'You know, one day they'll allow the Daily Insult in here,' he said.

I supposed that since they allowed Charlie in, anything was possible, but I didn't say so.

'Apologies, but I'm in a bit of a rush,' I said.

'Pity,' Charlie said. 'Wondered if you'd care for a rematch at snooker after our little tete-a-tete.'

'It'll have to be another time,' I said. 'So, what can you tell me?'

We were interrupted by the steward bringing two brandies.

'Put it on Mr Manner's tab,' Charlie said, and I nodded agreement. After all this was a desperate gamble.

'So, what's it all about?' I asked, as I found myself taking a mouthful of brandy that was rather too large for comfort. 'Not another commission on civic engagement?'

'Better. Or worse, depending on your pension. Word is, he's considering a second Brexit referendum. Wants to call it a "clarification exercise."'

I felt the blood drain from my face.

'You can't be serious.'

'I never joke about referendums, Guy. Not after the last one.'

'But why now?'

'Desperate for growth dear boy. They've tried and failed at everything else. Put a real dampener on the economy. The economist chappies reckon that being part of the single market and customs union is worth eighty billion a year to the economy, the government take is half of that. Fills their "soi disant" black hole at a stroke.'

'But it's political suicide,' I said, recalling the horror of it all.

'Word is the PM wants to prime the pump, spread a bit of cash to the red wall constituencies, promote all things European, soften us all up, make it a sort of fait accompli when it comes.'

So, that was why the hush hush push for money. It all started to make sense. I looked at Charlie. There had been occasions he'd been wrong, like the time he thought the government were going to re-establish a colonial office, but more than nine times out of ten he was right.

'The word is that you're being asked to cut the police budget to grease the Brexit wheels.'

How did he know that? I tried hard to look non-committal.

'Don't worry dear boy. This one's on us. The Daily Insult owners have a soft spot for the boys in blue. We'll run an article that shows how efficient they are.'

I didn't comment about the lack of gender sympathy or whatever it was. I was far too focused on the fact that this gift must come at a price.

'So, how can I help you Charlie?'

'Chalk it up to the ledger, dear boy. I shall expect something juicy in due course.'

'Charlie, you are a gentleman,' I said, raising my glass to him. 'Xiu Mei is a lucky lady.'

Back at the office I called in on George.

'Well?' George asked.

'Very,' I said. 'I think we may have a solution to our problem.'

'I'm listening,' George said, and he was. He even sat back in his chair twiddling a pencil between his fingers.

'It might be wise for the PM to put a halt on the idea of a Brexit referendum.'

The pencil twiddling stopped. So, it was true after all.

'Go on,'

'Word has it that the Daily Insult are running an article on how efficient the police are.'

'But they won't mention anything about another Brexit referendum?'

'That's about the size of it.'

A slow smile spread across George's face and the pencil was placed gently on the desk.

'A deus ex machina, Guy. Well done—public interest and all that.'

'Thank you,' I said. I considered adding that it might be better described as a deus ex tabloid but refrained from doing so.

I took the report on police waste and handed it with relief to the archivist for permanent filing and when I arrived home that night I was met by a windowsill full of scented geraniums—a gift, Ruth told me with a smile, from Monty—and I was reminded of another Disraeli quote "Success is the child of audacity."

Inclusivity

I think it was my old friend, Graham Carstairs, who, with the benefit of a lifetime spent abroad, described the United Kingdom as a global City with a second-rate country attached. Struck me as a bit harsh at the time, but with a few notable exceptions; Glyndebourne; Henley; Ascot, it has to be said that there isn't that much to entice your average patron of the arts, culture or even sport outside London. It was a topic of conversation that cropped up with another old friend, Anthony Belvoir, at the club a few weeks ago.

Frightful day, blowing a gale outside, and, as I wrestled manfully with my brolly, it was a second or two before I recognised the figure taking similar shelter from the storm.

'Anthony,' I said, as I handed my rather damp brolly to one of the young Polish girls the club now employs on reception, 'how the devil are you?'

'Tony,' he said.

'No, sorry dear boy, it's Guy,' I said, somewhat confused. Anthony was one of those bean counter chappies; recently retired as senior partner of a large City practise. I wondered whether all those debits and credits had unbalanced him.

'No, no, I know it's you Guy,' Anthony said, handing his brolly to the young girl, wiping an improbably youthful mop of hair from his eyes, and looking around as if to see if anyone else was listening, 'I'm Tony.'

'Of course you are, er, Tony,' I said, more confused than ever.

Anthony leaned forward rather conspiratorially, 'it's about inclusivity.'

'It is?' I asked.

'It is,' Anthony said. 'Look, let me buy you lunch, and I'll tell you all about it.'

We headed for the Dining Room and took a table by the fireplace. A great shame that they no longer have open fires, but at least the hearth gave the illusion of warmth. Whilst we waited for the rather decent steak and kidney pie to arrive, Anthony order a bottle of the St Emilion.

'You remember Blaire Cornwall?' Anthony asked.

I recalled the attractive young American woman at Merton who got into hot water with the University authorities for wearing her student gown in public. A bit ironic really as that was all she was wearing at the time. Had her photo in one of the newspapers under a typically inaccurate heading: "Blaire Bares All." Narrowly avoided getting sent down. Made quite a bit of money from it by all accounts and went to work as an arts correspondent.

'How could I forget,' I said.

'Quite,' Anthony said, blushing somewhat too readily and clearing his throat. 'Anyway, Blaire got me involved in this Central Arts thing.'

'Central Arts thing?'

'You know, funding the arts,' he leaned forwards, 'inclusivity is the in thing. Blaire gave me the nod; thought Anthony was a bit exclusive, that I should go for something simple. They all do it. So, I've lost the Ant and become Tony.' He paused, 'old Berty Gainsborough is on the board of trustees as well. You remember Berty?'

I pictured Berty; a keen member of the Officer Training Corps who had gone into the Navy.

'Have to call him Bob,' Anthony said.

'Indeed,' I said, trying to square the image of Admiral Gainsborough as "Bob"'. 'So, what exactly do you do?'

Anthony went a bit pale. 'They needed someone who could help with the financial side.' He took a gulp of the St. Emilion. 'Truth is it's a nightmare. They haven't got a clue about money.' He poured himself another large glass and ordered a second bottle. 'It's all about artistic integrity.' He shook his head, 'if you make a suggestion or ask for a business plan all you get is a blank look and then a lecture on how it would compromise the artistic integrity of the scheme.'

I took a sip of the St Emilion, a rather splendid Grand Cru Classé that was a work of art in itself.

Anthony seemed a trifle absorbed and so I helped myself to another glass as two steaming plates of steak and kidney pie arrived.

'So, what exactly do they expect you to do?' I asked, tucking into the pie. The club chef makes the best steak and kidney pies in London; they tell me that the secret is to add a dash of Worcester sauce to it, just gives it a little edge.

'I'm supposed to help assess the financial viability of the major projects.'

'I'd have thought that was right up your street.'

'So did I when I took the job on,' Anthony put his knife and fork down, his shoulders sagging, 'but it's like trying to count fog. I'll give you an example: A couple of years ago they came up with this arts and community centre in the Midlands; big yellow and green thing. Central Arts put £32 million into it; when the audit office looked at it last year it turns out five times as many people just use the public conveniences than actually go to the exhibitions. It costs the local council £2m a year,' he picked up his knife and fork and chewed slowly on some of the pie, 'works out at about £100 a pee,' he said, 'turned out they'd made no assessment of the likely demand; nothing.'

I savoured a little of the St Emilion.

'So why did it go ahead?'

'Politics dear boy,' he looked at me. 'More your sort of patch than mine. Central Arts are desperate to find projects outside London to support. Terribly bad form if it looks as if the rest of the country are subsidising London. They have to make sure that the majority of the funding goes to schemes outside the M25.'

'And does it?' I asked.

'They managed 50.8% last year,' he prodded at the steak and kidney pie. 'Thing is, all the really good stuff, you know like the Opera, Ballet, well it's all in London and if we didn't put a chunk of money in that direction you'd be paying over £500 a ticket. It might cut down on the number of poor people who come.'

Never really been my thing, Ballet, or Opera for that matter. Always full of improbable plots where the overweight high-pitched chap always gets the girl, but only after the deep voiced johnny has been bumped off. Odd how a chap with a dagger in his gizzards can sing for so long. Still, each to their own, or *a ciascuno il suo* as your average opera character might say.

'We may have the biggest nightmare yet in Stratford,' Anthony said, holding up his glass of wine and staring gloomily into its depths.

'Stratford?' I asked, thinking of the Olympic Park.

'Keep up Guy,' Anthony said, 'you know; Stratford-upon-Avon; small place in the Midlands, birthplace of Shakespeare and all that.'

'Oh yes,' I said. 'The new theatre.'

'I'm told the bard moved to London as soon as he got the chance,' Anthony said, raising his glass as if to drink, 'wouldn't go back to Stratford even when the plague closed all the theatres in London. Don't blame him, the town's like a blasted theme park; Mary Arden's; Anne Hathaway's; The Birthplace; New Place; Hall's Croft. Shops full of Shakespeare mugs; T-shirts; Tea towels; even some dreadful toys called Teddy Bards; you can imagine the sort of thing. Pretty ghastly really, but the Americans lap it up, all that culture stuff. At least that's what they keep telling me.' He took another large gulp of wine, his hand a trifle unsteady, then looked at me. 'Anyway, the theatre's too important to fail, as the current jargon has it.' He swirled the remaining wine around in his glass, downed it in one and placed the glass firmly on the tablecloth, fingers still holding the stem. 'Look, Guy, I'd value your opinion. I get tickets all the time that I can't use. Why don't you and Ruth pop up and see one of the performances, tell me what you think about the place?'

At the time it seemed like a good idea. I could remember as a child being taken to Stratford to see Twelfth Night; sitting in comfortable armchairs watching Malvolio strut his stuff in yellow cross gartered stockings; and, as Ruth loves Shakespeare, I might earn a few brownie points as the Americans would indelicately say. Good to his word, Anthony came up with tickets to an evening performance of Henry V.

'We'll go up by train,' I said to Ruth, as I handed over the envelope for her to inspect, and explained Anthony's predicament.

'That'll take far too long,' Ruth said, looking dubiously at the tickets, 'it's a Saturday night, travelling back on a Sunday will be a nightmare. I've got a bridge match that Sunday evening.'

'That's no problem,' I said, a little surprised at the less than enthusiastic reaction, 'we'll drive up. It'll only take a couple of hours, and we can be back just after midnight,' I said, adding in my best theatrical Shakespearean, 'you shall be my hope, my stay, my guide and lantern to my feet.' Following up my rhetorical flourish with a courtly bow.

'Don't be silly Guy,' Ruth pursed her lips over the slightest hint of a smile, and tapped the tickets against her chin, 'alright,' she said finally, 'but you're driving..'

'Think on thy Guy, when thou haply seest some rare, noteworthy object in thy travel,' I said.

'Enough Guy,' Ruth said, 'anyway I think that's Two Gentlemen of Verona.

The journey wasn't that bad, but we spent ages trying to find somewhere to park. You would have thought that £75 million of public money might have bought a car park, but apparently not and so we trudged through the streets from a municipal car park, taking in a range of aromas, that suggested an inadequate supply of public conveniences and an oversupply of burger bars, as we did so. In the gloom I could make out some of the familiar façade of the theatre as I remembered it from my youth but now accompanied by a glass and girder construction with one of those towers that firemen use for practice and drying out their hoses bolted onto the side.

'It looks quite smart,' Ruth said, 'probably has quite a good view up there.'

Inside it was clear the builders gave up on finishing the thing, just painted over some of the walls. You could even see some of the original wiring dangling from the remnants of old plaster.

'It's got a real creative feel,' Ruth said, 'I like it.'

I looked carefully to see if she was quite alright; mad as hatters some of the cousins on her mother's side.

The bell went and we hurried to get to our seats. Gone were the comfortable armchairs. We were cheek by jowl in what felt like a sunken pit two rows back from a stage that towered above us. Gone too were the elegant swept circle and balcony replaced by girders, bolted together like some giant Meccano set, which appeared to block the view of a good many people.

'Isn't this marvellous?' Ruth said, 'so easy to get to your seat, and we're so close to the stage.'

I wedged my knees into the limited space available as the elderly gentleman immediately in front of me fiddled with a hearing aid. To my surprise the old boy then produced an electronic ear horn from inside his jacket pocket for good measure. As he stuck the horn to his ear, and turned the volume up on both implements, they generated a quite remarkable whining noise that was to recur periodically throughout the performance. I looked round at Ruth, but she was hiding behind her programme.

Chorus stood solemnly on stage, although I could only see his feet without straining my neck.

'O for a muse of fire,' Chorus began, 'that would ascend the brightest heaven of invention.'

I settled down to absorb the introduction whilst the old boy in front of me fiddled with his hearing apparatus. He finally gave up as the first scene came to a close and Henry appeared on stage.

As Henry turned to face stage right and it became harder to hear him, the old boy leaned over to an elderly lady on his left, who, it turned out was his wife, and in a loud American accent asked, 'What are they doing now?'

His good lady paused for thought and then said in a subdued tone, 'Well, they're off to fight the French dear.'

Apparently satisfied with this explanation the old boy straightened, and, after a little further adjustment of the ear horn that waved in front of me like the head of a triffid on steroids, settled down to watch some of the play.

As Henry swept off stage at the end of the first act, the old boy put down his ear horn, as if retracting a periscope, and turned to his wife. 'What are they doing now?'

His wife paused for thought, perhaps deciding whether to respond or ask him to pipe down, but then said, 'Well, they're off to fight the French dear.'

The ear horn rose once more and turned as if scanning for vulnerable merchant shipping.

'Have you heard that American?' I asked Ruth as we queued for a drink at the interval.

'Rather sweet isn't it,' Ruth said. 'Quite brave to come out when you can't hear that well.'

There are times when I wonder if Ruth is on quite the right wavelength.

'A cappuccino and a latte please,' I said as we finally reached the head of the queue.

'Don't do cappuccino or latte,' said a puffy young woman with a broad Birmingham accent. 'Takes too long.'

'I'll just have a filter coffee,' Ruth said, leaning across me and smiling at the young woman who smiled back.

'I'll have the same please,' I said, and in the absence of anywhere to sit, we stood standing as we sipped our lukewarm, cardboard tasting coffee. I had managed to finish half of the dubious brew when the final bell went. Somewhat relieved to leave the coffee unfinished, we headed back into the theatre.

As Henry V girded his loins and I looked forward to the Harfleur speech, the old boy leaned over to his wife once more. 'What are they doing now?' he asked.

His wife took a longer pause than before, giving Henry a chance to get as far as *summoning up the blood* before replying. 'Well, they're off to fight the French dear.'

This time the old boy looked as if he required further explanation, but his wife's gentle hand on his arm seemed to stall any such request for a while, and the ear horn resumed its surveillance.

Agincourt won, Henry triumphant and settling down to the difficult task of wooing the French Princess Katherine, the old boy sought fit to garner some clarification.

'Is that the English King?' he asked.

'Well yes dear,' came the reply.

'But he said he was French,' the old boy said, rather missing the whole point of the play.

Back in the car I thought it only right to elicit Ruth's views on the dreadful evening.

'It was wonderful,' Ruth said, 'I loved it, and I think the couple in front of us did too.'

'But he didn't understand a word of it,' I said.

'But she did.' Ruth turned to me. 'It's the most succinct precis of Henry V I've ever heard.'

'Hm,' I said. 'And the theatre. They've destroyed it.

Ruth gave me one of those odd looks. 'Don't be such a stick in the mud Guy, they have done no such thing. It's perfect. You're close to the stage; you see all the action; it's modern and comfortable,' she paused. 'You can tell Anthony that Central Arts have done a wonderful thing funding the new theatre,' she paused again. 'It's about inclusivity.'

A Matter of Trust

It was a Saturday and for once the government wasn't in crisis. Well, more precisely, some bright spark had redefined "crisis" so that anything short of World War Three now counted as an "exigency."

It would have been wonderful to think that this redefinition came about through a careful analysis of the meaning of the two words, but apparently it was because focus groups of the hoi polloi didn't regard the word "exigency" as alarming as "crisis."

Life on the domestic front was also tranquil. Ruth was in good humour. Out of the blue Sally Belvoir, her bridge partner and wife of Anthony, had invited us to attend an open-air performance of something at our local Heritage Trust pile that afternoon.

Garfield House was a rather splendid Tudor affair that had been home to a family of recusants with plenty of tortured ghosts to attest to their sacrifice for their faith and a gloriously chequered history in the civil war where the Garfields had managed to fight for both King and Parliament and made a packet in the process. Could have done with a few of them in government.

There was also, if memory served, a brief but lucrative interlude involving a sugar plantation in Barbados. I recalled Ruth reading out the official history of the place in which it was referred to as "an overseas agricultural venture." One of those euphemisms that litter our history books these days.

Ruth had been a volunteer for many years as had Sally Belvoir. You know the sort of thing: pointing out the limited facilities to desperate mothers and toddlers, explaining who Elizabeth I was to American tourists and why the cafeteria was closed again. It all seemed harmless enough and I was quite looking forward to a Pimms listening to a gentle performance of A Midsummer Night's Dream or some such.

Anyway, whilst the rest of the office were dealing with a number of exigencies, the absence of crises gave me the perfect excuse to take the weekend off and I popped into the Club for a coffee and a bit of peace.

I was in the library looking at the Times crossword. My own copy, I hasten to add—terribly bad form when chaps fill in the Club's paper. I was just mulling over ten across when Anthony Belvoir came in.

'Anthony,' I said, getting up to shake his hand.

'Tony,' he said.

'I thought…' I started to say, then recalled the conversation about the Arts Council and the importance of inclusive names. 'Still working for the Arts Council?'

'All a matter of hats,' Tony, or should I say, Anthony, said.

'Indeed?'

'But I may be donning a new one shortly.'

'I see,' I said, none the wiser. 'Can I get you a coffee of something?' Awfully decent of Sally to invite us to Garfield House. Appreciate it.'

'Ah yes, hmm. Actually, a coffee would hit the spot. And I could do with your help.'

'About hats?'

Anthony laughed. 'Well, in a kind of a way, yes. It's about a new hat I'm wearing.'

'This isn't to do with the Arts Council then?' I asked, thinking back to that dreadful evening in Stratford.

'Goodness gracious no. Well, yes, but no. Not exactly.' He wagged his head like a weathervane uncertain which way the wind was blowing. 'You remember I mentioned Blaire Cornwall?' He reddened.

'Indeed,' I said recalling once more Merton College's answer to Lady Godiva.

'Blaire said she could use my help at the Heritage Trust.'

So, that explained the Heritage Trust tickets and for the first time as I looked at Anthony I had a sense of unease.

'How on Earth did Blaire get involved with the Heritage Trust?'

'Some collaboration between the Arts Council and the Trust. Something to do with open-air theatre.' Anthony turned a deeper shade of burgundy.

It occurred to me that there was a metaphor in there about Blaire and open-air theatre, but looking at Anthony's obvious confusion about all things Blaire, I resisted the temptation to say so.

'Anyway,' Anthony continued. 'The thing is I've got to prepare an Impact Assessment Report.'

It was hard to imagine anything having an impact on the Heritage Trust. Mind you it was years since I'd been to one. Used to be all cream teas and thistles on the chairs to stop the great unwashed from sitting down anywhere. I must have looked blank.

'The Art's Council are putting in a chunk of money for those outdoor performances and community arts projects.'

'Anthony, I like art as much as the next man, and I'm looking forward to tonight, but…'

'Good heavens no. It's not the artistic merit of the thing that I'm worried about. It's the political fallout.'

'Politics not my bailiwick, old boy. The civil service have to stay strictly impartial.'

'I wouldn't expect anything else, Guy, but it seems that The Social Exclusion Committee want to be sure that cultural representation of projects funded by the Arts Council fit approved criteria and that heritage and historical narratives are consistent with government policy.'

As I choked on my coffee and struggled to land the cup safely on its saucer, I reflected that these were quite long words for Anthony, and I wondered whether he had been coached by someone.

'Are you alright?' Anthony asked as he jumped up and thumped my back. I nodded my head although I was anything but. The Social Exclusion Committee involvement meant that Poppy Grimsdyke had her teeth locked onto the Heritage Trust, and when she had a bone to play with it was generally unwise to come anywhere near.

'Anyway,' Anthony continued, taking my assurance of my health at face value. 'I'm a bit out of my depth. Better with numbers really.'

'You did say the Social Exclusion Committee,' I said when I managed to gasp out the words.

'You know about them?'

He said it in such an innocent way that I had to believe that he was genuinely new to La Grimsdyke and her fellow Valkyries that terrorised Committee Room seventeen and most of the upper committee corridor, swooping down from time to time to snatch some unsuspecting junior minister to grill.

'They play an important role in the Prime Minister's drive to bring balance to society.' I said with all the gravitas I could muster.

'Ah,' Anthony said with a nod of understanding. He glanced out of the window as if mulling it over and a puzzled look came over him, like someone who's just discovered they're in the wrong meeting. 'What exactly does that mean?'

'I think we can say that the Committee has a wide ranging and dare I say influential brief.'

'Hmm. Wide-ranging, influential...I see,' Anthony said, although it was clear he did not.

Everything in me screamed that I should make an exit, prise that afternoon's tickets from Ruth and burn them on the fire, before Poppy Grimsdyke found out that I had anything to do with whatever it was that Anthony was engaged in. But as I looked at Anthony I couldn't but help feel sympathy for a fellow traveller who had no conceivable idea as to the scale of the tsunami headed toward him.

That said, the Arts Council was hardly a bastion of tradition, and the Heritage Trust was not above promoting, shall we say, socially aware policies. There might be little scope for conflict even taking into account Poppy Grimsdyke's ability to turn a cream tea into a constitutional exigency, or should I say crisis.

'What exactly are these open-air performances? I thought they would be Shakespeare, maybe Marlowe at a pinch.'

'Well,' Anthony said. 'I've got tonight's programme.' He reached into his jacket pocket and handed it over to me.

The fact that he had a pristine copy to hand made me wonder again whether this had all been prepared in advance. I have an uncanny knack of sensing when trouble is brewing and my antennae were rattling around like Joe Root's bat in the dying light of the fifth day of a test match at Lord's—restless, poised, and haunted by his failure as England Captain. But as I looked at Anthony, it was hard to believe that the innocent look that I'd known ever since we were at school together could be contrived.

I looked at the programme. There was a tour of the house from four o'clock and various art displays that looked from the picture as if they might have been hung upside down, although it was difficult to tell. The main event was a performance by a group called the Rainbow Theatre Company.

The Tempest: Echoes of Inclusion
A site-specific reimagining of Shakespeare's final play, exploring the legacies of empire and the unheard voices of the land.

The tingling of my antennae became uncomfortable, but for the life of me I couldn't see why this would be of interest let alone concern to Poppy Grimsdyke. In fact, it was right up her street. She would approve of the inhabitants of Prospero's Island led by Caliban rising up against their oppressors, casting off their collective yoke and no doubt demanding reparations for the next few centuries.

I scanned through the programme.

'And this is being funded by the Arts Council?'

'Well, yes,' Anthony said. 'And no.'

'No?'

'The Faversham Foundation are supporting the Arts Council and they're using that money for this.' He pointed at the brochure.

'You mean Henry Faversham is funding a revisionist play about slavery?'

The whole idea was so absurd that it was difficult not to laugh. Sir Henry Faversham of all people. A Times Rich List regular, Chairman, not Chair, of the Heritage Preservation Council devoted to protecting Britain's historical integrity, Deputy Lord Lieutenant of one of the Shires and funder, it was rumoured, of a number of political causes that would have given Poppy Grimsdyke seizures. Worse he was a cousin of Ruth's on her mother's side. The dark side as Private Eye once described, with more malice than I thought was strictly necessary.

'You know him too?' Anthony asked. 'Sally said there was some connection with Ruth, said she'd sit her next to him tonight.'

'You mean he's coming to the performance at Garfield House?'

'Well, yes. It's the opening night you see. They're all coming. You know, Blaire, Poppy Grimsdyke, Henry Faversham…'

'You mean Poppy Grimsdyke is going to spend an evening with Henry Faversham?'

'Well, yes. Blaire thought it would be a good idea to get all the major stakeholders' perspectives. You know, for the Impact Assessment Report. Is that a problem?'

'Is Blaire sound? I mean she hasn't taken to baying at the moon or anything?'

'I think that's rather offensive and uncalled for, Guy. You never did have a good opinion of Blaire.'

Everything in me wanted to shake some sense into him.

'Do you know what happens if you store fireworks next to a bonfire?'

Anthony looked puzzled. 'Well, I suppose they might explode.'

'That is exactly what Blaire is doing by putting Poppy Grimsdyke anywhere near Henry Faversham.'

'But why would she do that?' Anthony asked in a tone that defied guile.

I ran through the excuses I could make. Perhaps I could develop a sudden case of dysentery or have a spontaneous mental breakdown. Maybe an exigency at the office that suddenly became a full-blown crisis.

But as I ran through the list of possible exit strategies, Anthony delivered what in jousting terms is described as the coup de mort.

'After all,' he said with the look of someone mulling over a mouthful of fudge. 'The Prime Minister's going as well. Been invited by the Chair of the Heritage Trust. Blaire wouldn't want a scene if he's there. Would she?'

I left Anthony and the club in something of a haze. I was going to be witness to a full-blown spat in front of the Prime Minister. George would never forgive me. But then why hadn't George told me that the Prime Minister was going?

I raced over to the Cabinet Office.

'What are you doing here?' George asked. 'I thought you were taking the day off.'

'I was, I am. I mean…why didn't you tell me that the PM is going to Garfield House this afternoon?'

'Ah,' George said. 'Need to know basis. Trying to keep it low key so that the evening doesn't get totally overrun with security-wallahs galumphing around the park.'

'Does Blaire Cornwall know.'

'I imagine so. Why do you ask?'

'She's only invited Poppy Grimsdyke and Henry Faversham.'

There was silence. I watched the blood slowly drain from George's face.

'What on Earth is she playing at?'

'Can't you stop it George? Find something important for the PM to do like open a kindergarten or something.'

'Let me try.'

I watched George call the PM's secretary and heard the slight tremor in his voice as he explained that it would be wise for the PM to make other arrangements. Then with a shake of his head he slowly put the phone down.

'No can do, Guy. Seems the PM promised his wife they'd go.'

'This is a disaster,' I said. 'What are we going to do?'

'You mean what are you going to do, Guy. I've got a plateful of exigencies here. I'm relying on you to make sure that the PM isn't embarrassed tonight.'

I hurried home in the hope of catching Ruth and persuading her that it was time to pack our bags and disappear to Tristan da Cunha (which the last time I looked was the remotest inhabited place on Earth)

at least until the storm blew over and we could
survey the wreckage from a safe distance.

'Hello Guy,' she said in that half-distracted way
she has when trying on her finery. 'What do you
think?' She had laid two outfits on the bed, a long
dress that looked like it came from one of those
nature brochures that remind you of moss and
stagnant ponds, and something that looked vaguely
like a costume from a lugubrious Edwardian
melodrama topped off with her mother's brooch
and a silver necklace.

'They both look wonderful,' I said. 'I'm not sure
that I'm not developing a migraine.'

'Don't be ridiculous Guy. You don't get
migraines.' She came a little closer. 'You haven't
been drinking have you?'

'Certainly not,' I said.

'Don't get any ideas of weaselling out of this
afternoon. I'm looking forward to it. I haven't seen
Henry for ages and Sally told me Stephanie's
going…'

'Stephanie?' The reference to the PM's wife
caught me by surprise. Did everyone know the PM
was going to be there?

'Stephanie, Guy. You know, the Prime
Minister's wife. The man you're supposed to serve.
I'm looking forward to catching up with her. I don't
get to see much of her these days. Besides,' she
said, turning to consider the dresses on the bed once

more. 'Sally invited us, and I've agreed we'll go. It's the least we can do to support Anthony.'

'But…'

'I've decided, Guy, so go and get changed. And don't put on that old blazer, wear something sensible.'

The taxi seemed far too keen to get us to Garfield House, and as the great pile came into sight I wondered how those recusants must have felt as they saw Walsingham's agents searching out hidden Jesuits ready to throw them in the Tower and have them racked or even hanged drawn and quartered. I wondered too whether there were any secret priest holes in which I too could find sanctuary.

'Guy, Ruth,' a rich deep voice boomed out as we stepped out of the taxi. Henry Faversham bounded up and swept Ruth up in a bear hug. 'How's my favourite cousin?' He asked holding her at arm's length and studying her much as one might a rag doll.

'It's lovely to see you, Harry,' Ruth said. For once there was a slight hint of concern in her voice. 'Is Phoenicia here?' She asked looking around.

'Powdering her nose in the left turret,' Henry laughed at his own attempt at humour and Ruth looked more relaxed as she saw Phoenicia appear from the shadows of the building like something dreamt up by Bram Stoker. She gave Ruth a broad smile and a peculiar wave.

'Looking forward to this afternoon?' She said, the smile if anything broader still.

'Very much,' Ruth said, giving her a hug and an air kiss. 'Wouldn't miss it for the world.'

I took a nervous look around for Poppy Grimsdyke, but there was no sign of her and nor could I discern the sound of her laugh. I wondered whether it would be possible to keep Poppy and Henry apart during the evening, but avoiding Henry's inevitable explosion during the play would be impossible. Perhaps it would be better to have the confrontation between Poppy and Henry first, get it out of the way before the PM arrived. But my hope that timing might work for me was dashed by the arrival of the PM's car and a small cavalcade of black Range Rovers.

Blaire appeared from nowhere to stand in front of the imposing entrance to Garfield House as the cavalcade drew up right beside her.

I saw the PM's wife give Ruth and Phoenicia a small wave and then we were bustled into the great hall. I found myself next to Henry Faversham.

'You a frequenter of Heritage Trust properties, Henry?'

'Not at the moment,' he said gazing up at the forest of hand-carved oak beams soaring overhead, held together by enough joinery to build a small ship. 'Lost their way a bit. You know, all this rewilding of perfectly decent agricultural land, rainbow lanyards and compost in the cafeterias.'

'Compost?' I asked wondering for a moment if he was thinking of the garden centres attached to the ubiquitous Heritage Trust kitchen garden.

'You know, inedible stuff they serve, leaves and such. Some nonsense about having most of the menu plant based. I think you know Dicky Pennington. He leases a bit of land from the Heritage Trust. They cancelled his contract for eggs of all things. Doesn't affect Dicky that much, but he tells me a lot of Heritage Trust tenants feel betrayed. And as for…'

I saw him take a deep breath as he was about to launch into some diatribe, but the tour of the house was pressing on and the stampede to keep up with the Prime Minister curtailed our conversation.

Looking for all the world like a latter day Boudica, Poppy Grimsdyke materialised next to the Prime Minister and had him by the arm, no doubt lecturing him that it was Tudor women who ruled the kingdom and wielded the power and should be recognised as such in history books.

I became separated from Ruth but saw her close to the PM's group. She was giggling in a very un-Ruth like way with Sally Belvoir, Phoenicia Faversham, Blaire Cornwall and the PM's wife.

Henry Faversham was getting closer to Poppy Grimsdyke by the second and I wondered whether I could break the glass on one of the fire alarms, but there was no chance of getting close. I heard snippets from the guide 'Sir William Garfield…window Latin motto…loyalty, empire…' I saw Poppy raise an eyebrow and cling on tighter to the PM, but she seemed to let it wash over her.

We all trooped past a blur of Garfield family portraits and a positive minefield of contentious antiquities: Lady Margaret's exhortation to her fellow wives to be obedient and fruitful, a Heritage Trust display of how they were decolonialising Garfield House, but by some miracle we found ourselves out into the gardens and in front of a stage, searching for our allocated seats without any incident having occurred. Perhaps there was a God after all, I thought.

I saw Phoenicia Faversham take a firm grip of Henry's arm as they sat in the front row, mercifully at the other end from Poppy Grimsdyke who was still bending the PM's ear in strident terms. I tried to listen, something about Tudor feminism, the inappropriateness of the term recusant and the implied blight on the true faith.

There was an unfamiliar brightness in Ruth's eyes as she sat next to me in the front row. 'So, nice to see everyone, Guy. We don't come out enough. We should do this more often.'

I was about to say that I wasn't sure my nerves would stand it, but the re-imagining of The Tempest started at that moment. I struggled to follow the revised version, but it seemed that Prospera an exiled African Princess who escaped from the clutches of the British rallied the enslaved islanders. Using Voodoo and help from the non-binary spirit Ariel, they wreaked revenge on the British by driving their ships onto the rocks and enslaving them. There was a complicated scene about freeing the British in return for reparations that I didn't entirely understand.

Throughout my heart was pounding. I could see that Poppy Grimsdyke was lapping it up. The PM appeared indifferent and along the row Henry Faversham was wearing what I can only describe as a self-satisfied smile. It didn't make sense.

Then the show was over, and Henry buttonholed me. 'Just wanted to say thank you to your good lady. You're a lucky chap, Guy.' Then he laughed. 'And I always thought bridge was such a dull game.' Then the PM was gone and so was Henry.

I blinked. For a moment I couldn't place the comment about bridge, but then it came to me—Ruth's bridge nights. I knew Sally Belvoir belonged to the club, but I'd never paid that much attention to the others.

'What just happened there?' I asked as we got into the taxi.

Ruth laughed and I watched as she waved goodbye to Sally Belvoir and Blaire Cornwall.

'That was priceless,' Ruth said.

'I don't understand.'

'Sally told me there might be a bit of a storm tonight, if you'll forgive the pun. So, we took steps.'

'Who took steps? What steps?'

'I couldn't let Harry be embarrassed. The poor dear. He's been so generous with his money. And Stephanie didn't want the PM embarrassed either, none of us did. I'm sure George probably told you to make sure he wasn't.'

'But Henry sat like a lamb right the way through all that…' I struggled to find the right words to describe the re-imagining of Shakespeare's last play.

'That was Stephanie's idea. It turns out that the Chair of the Heritage Trust is up for election next month and Stephanie knows the trustees. I think Harry will make an excellent Chair don't you?' She laughed. 'Might get something decent to eat in the cafeterias, you never know.'

'But why didn't you tell me?'

'And miss all the fun of watching your face. It was the best theatre I've seen in years.'

I stared out of the taxi window watching the familiar streets of Richmond coming into sight. I recalled a Disraeli quote "A female friend, amiable, clever, and devoted, is a possession more valuable than parks and palaces; and without such a muse, few men can succeed in life, none be contented." He probably knew Ruth in another life.

'Well, I hope I provided some entertainment,' I said with as much grace as I could muster.

Ruth put her hand on mind. 'I'm teasing, Guy. I would have told you if I'd had time. I was only sure it would all work when I got the nod from Phoenicia. Besides, I didn't want to turn a Shakespeare drama into an exigency.'

www.ingramcontent.com/pod-product-compliance
Lightning Source LLC
Chambersburg PA
CBHW032019180726
48283CB00008B/2754